Joss heard a sound that drowned everything out.

She'd been dreading a terrible incident and now one was happening. The gang was after agents and innocent people. And somehow she felt as if she could have prevented this.

A powerful engine revved. She looked up. The vertical blinds were closed over her apartment's sliding glass doors, but a bright light flashed through the crevices— as if someone was shining a spotlight on the doors. The engine revved closer, like it was just below Joss's window...

Rapid gunfire exploded through the air. Bullets shattered the glass doors, ripping across the entire apartment.

Joss flung herself flat. Bullets tore across the room, destroying everything in their path. They zinged over her head...straight down the hall toward Dylan's running figure.

She screamed his name before another round shredded through the apartment, sending splinters everywhere...

Tanya Stowe is a Christian fiction author with an unexpected edge. She is married to the love of her life, her high school sweetheart. They have four children and twenty-one grandchildren, a true adventure. She fills her books with the unusual—mysteries and exotic travel, even a murder or two. No matter where Tanya takes you—on a trip to foreign lands or a suspenseful journey packed with danger—be prepared for the extraordinary.

Books by Tanya Stowe

Love Inspired Suspense

Mojave Rescue
Fatal Memories

FATAL MEMORIES

TANYA STOWE

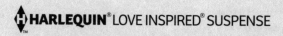

HARLEQUIN® LOVE INSPIRED® SUSPENSE

Recycling programs
for this product may
not exist in your area.

 LOVE INSPIRED BOOKS

ISBN-13: 978-1-335-23236-6

Fatal Memories

Copyright © 2019 by Tanya Stowe

Printed in U.S.A.

Persecuted, but not forsaken;
cast down, but not destroyed.
—2 Corinthians 4:9

For my dad, who showed me the wonders of Arizona.

ONE

Crawl! The woman woke slowly.

Wake up and crawl!

She tried to move, tried to obey the thought that was so insistent, almost desperate. She lifted her head half an inch off the ground. Viselike pain gripped her temples and she groaned out loud. She froze, trying to ease the agony, but it didn't go away. Now it pierced like sharp blades…her eyes, her temples, the back of her head.

It hurt so much, she collapsed…breathed in dust and grit. She coughed. The pain split her head in two and she cried out again.

Where was she? Why was she on the ground?

Crawl! Crawl away or you'll die!

That's right. The tunnel. She had to get out. Now.

Unable to lift her head without piercing agony, she slid one leg upwards and pushed her body along the ground. The grit scraped her cheek as she moved. No matter. She had to get away.

Raising one hand, she pulled herself a little farther.

After a moment she was able to coordinate her hands with her legs. She pushed and pulled herself inch by inch, through the tunnel. Her head throbbed with blinding agony. Her cheek burned and still she crawled forward, driven by fear of what lay behind her. She had to get away.

She dared to look up. Pain shot through her head. Light. Light just ahead!

A click echoed behind her.

Too late! An explosion rocked the darkness. The shock wave slammed her head onto the gritty ground and she slipped into darkness again.

The headache returned. Or maybe it had never left. She couldn't remember. It pierced her head like an ax… right between the eyes. And the spinning. She might be awake, but the world was moving around and around, even with her eyes closed. Her body ached from head to toe. Something was pumping cool air through her nose. The rest of her body felt hot, stiff. Impossible to move. Afraid to open her eyes, she held perfectly still, waiting…hoping the world would stop shifting around her.

Wait…someone was singing. Soft, low, smooth as velvet. Beautiful. What was the song? An old hymn. She heard "saved a wretch like me."

Strong and firm, that voice. Low but not too low. Comfortable. A bit familiar but she couldn't quite give it a face. Couldn't remember the name. Who was it?

She tried to speak, but all that came out was a groan. The singing stopped.

Someone grasped her hand. "Joss? Can you hear me, Joss?"

Joss? The name felt reassuring. She tried to lick her lips, but her mouth was so dry, her tongue stuck. Something cool, a dripping, welcome moisture, ran over her lips. Liquid slipped in, onto her tongue, easing the tight, dry feeling.

"More."

"Here you go." The voice without a face swabbed her lips again. The moisture eased the stickiness. Made it easier to talk.

"Hurts."

"What hurts, Joss?"

"My head."

"That's because you have a concussion. A pretty serious one. You're in the hospital."

A hospital. She wasn't in danger anymore. Someone was taking care of her. Maybe the man with the gentle, kind…safe voice. She wanted to curl into the safety of that strong voice and sleep. If only she could put a face to it. Maybe if she opened her eyes…

Her lids felt as dry as her lips. Like sandpaper. And the glimmer of light caused the ax to sink deeper into her skull. She squeezed her eyes shut again.

"Go easy, Joss. There's no hurry." But his tone held a thread of something that said there was. Impatience? Frustration or worry? What was it?

She opened her eyes again, just a slit. The light didn't hurt as much this time. Didn't create the blinding pain. She waited a moment, then opened them all the way. His face was above her. Curly brown hair, a bit long. The shadow of a dark beard. He needed a shave. A slightly Roman nose. Not prominent. Just strong. A hooded brow over hazel eyes, more green than brown. His eyes almost matched the color of the collared sweater he wore. A slight frown creased his forehead.

Worry. Definitely worry she'd heard in his voice. Worry for her. That was a nice thought. As she studied him, the frown eased and he smiled. "It's good to see you back."

Back. Where had she been?

She licked her lips. "What happened?"

"There was a cave-in. You were trapped in the tunnel."

"A tunnel? What was I doing in a tunnel?"

The frown returned. "I was hoping you could tell *me*."

She tried to shake her head but it hurt. Instead she closed her eyes and tried to think. To picture a tunnel. But all she could see was the gray mist behind her closed eyes. "I—I don't remember a tunnel…or a cave-in."

She heard him inhale slowly. "That's all right. It's normal not to remember the details of an accident. It's the brain's way of healing."

Normal. This didn't feel normal. It felt empty. Scary. There was nothing beyond the gray mist. Nothing. Not even a memory of the handsome face at her bedside.

"Who…are…you?"

His features went slack with surprise before he gathered himself. "I'm Dylan. Dylan Murphy. We met about a month ago, when I came here from DC."

She swallowed hard. Nothing he said pierced the fog in her brain. "Where is *here*?"

"Tucson. We're in Tucson."

He didn't attempt to hide his concern now. He stared at her.

Panic built inside her. Her gaze shot around the room, trying to find something familiar, something she knew. Nothing rang a bell. It all seemed strange and foreign.

Dylan gripped her hand. "Stay calm, Joss. It's all right."

She shook her head in spite of the pain. "It's not all right. Nothing's right. I can't remember an accident or anything about Tucson. I don't know who you are. You called me Joss, but I don't know my last name." Her head pounded with renewed force, so she squeezed her eyes shut. "I can't remember anything!"

Hot tears leaked out from her tightly squeezed eyes and ran down her face. A soft finger wiped the tears off her cheek, and his voice pierced through the pounding inside her head. "It's all right, Joss. I'm here. I remember, and I won't leave until you do too."

His words slid into her heart and loosened the tight band of fear that threatened to crush it. She gripped his hand as she slipped into the fog.

Dylan Murphy took a slow, calming breath and tried again.

"Look, Holmquist." The other man was actually a special-operation supervisor for the border patrol. Dylan was a drug-enforcement agent, on special assignment from Washington, DC. He'd been back in Tucson for over a month now, and so far working with Holmquist and his agents had been a piece of cake…until yesterday, when Jocelyn Walker had disappeared.

Things had changed drastically, and now Dylan would have to fall back on his position as the tough hard-liner, the role that had earned him his reputation. He didn't have any other choice.

When they'd first brought Joss in, he'd been so concerned with her survival, the possibility of her losing her memory had never occurred to him. This was a new wrinkle…one that had initially thrown him for a loop.

He didn't want to believe Joss was guilty, but she couldn't remember what had happened, and the cold, hard facts were undeniable. Dylan had to face them… and had to force her coworkers to do the same.

"You have to put in a request for a search warrant. We need to get into Officer Walker's apartment to see what we can find."

The supervisor turned to face him, his dark features growing darker. "Find? Exactly what do you think you're going to find in *my* officer's home?"

Dylan inhaled. "I don't know. That's why we have to get in there."

Holmquist's features hardened. "What's the rush? If Officer Walker survives, she'll be in this hospital bed for a long time."

"I agree. Long enough for her partners…" All of the border-patrol officers standing around the hospital waiting room turned abruptly. Dylan raised his hands. "*If*—I repeat *if*—she has partners in crime…they will have ample opportunity to clean out any evidence."

Holmquist looked as if he were about to explode. "I

don't care how special the Drug Enforcement Administration thinks you are, *Special* Agent Murphy, you have no right to come in here, accusing one of my best officers of a criminal act."

"I'm sorry, sir, but she *was* found in a collapsed tunnel beneath the Nogales border, with a stash of heroin worth five thousand dollars."

"I know how it looks!" The officer's raised voice reverberated around the quiet room before the man halted. Fisting his hand, he shook it loose and looked around. "Let's go someplace where we can discuss this more calmly."

He spun and stalked away. Dylan followed. He didn't look at the men and women around him—anger and bitter resentment would be reflected on every face. Jocelyn Walker was popular with her fellow officers. Despite the fact the twenty-seven-year-old had risen through the ranks rapidly, much faster than some of her older counterparts, she had managed to maintain a good rapport with most of her coworkers. Competent, eager to learn, outgoing and humble, she had earned their respect without a problem.

She'd earned Dylan's as well. He'd liked her from the beginning and they'd developed a teasing banter that made working together pleasant. It didn't hurt that she had a winning smile, silky, long black hair and the prettiest gray eyes Dylan had ever seen. Her beauty certainly turned his head the first time he'd met her. But he refused to let it get in the way of his investigation. As far as he could tell, her looks had not earned her special attention in the force. It just made the over-all package of Agent Walker easy to take.

As soon as his suspicions began to take form, he knew he was going to have a hard time convincing her supervisor—or any of her coworkers—that she might be involved with the gang he'd been sent to Tucson to investigate.

Holmquist stopped at the coffee machine and punched in his order. A cup slid down and black coffee poured into it. The swishing, pouring sound echoed through the taut, conspicuous silence in the waiting room. When it finished, the captain removed his coffee and, without a word to Dylan, stalked through the hall, past the nurses station, to the elevators.

Dylan followed silently, suspecting the man needed time to gain control of his temper. They reached the bottom floor and walked outside. Even at 2:00 a.m., the emergency room was crowded. Holmquist crossed to the opposite curb of the parking lot, where it was quiet and the lights not so bright. He stepped over the curb, to the rock-filled interior of the divider, where he stopped and took a sip of his coffee.

Dylan waited and stared at the lightning crackling across the distant night sky.

August. Monsoon season in Southern Arizona, when storms from the Gulf of California sweep up from Baja to bathe the desert in torrential downpours. One minute everything was dry, and the next a deluge soaked the parched earth. The desert turned green and cacti blossomed with bright blooms. Everything turned brilliant and bright. Dylan hated to admit it, but it was beautiful.

And the skies… Light or dark, the skies were always spectacular. Lightning would rip the clouds open, and thunder would rock the earth. This season, and all that came with it, was one of the things he'd missed about home. Probably the only thing.

He shook his head with an abrupt gesture, stopping the memories before they could flood in. "Look, I don't want to think that one of our own could be guilty."

Holmquist shook his head. The olive green of his uniform almost disappeared in the night, but the bright yellow lettering of his name and border-patrol patches stood out in the light from the entrance across the way. "Joss is not one of yours. She's my officer and I don't believe I could be that wrong about her. After fifteen years in the US Border Patrol, I know people." He turned to Dylan, his features set. "I know *my* people."

Dylan shrugged. "You said she hasn't been her normal self. We've all noticed that she's been off track, different for the past week—distracted and lost in her own thoughts. Now she shows up in the middle of a drug shipment, beneath a cave-in."

"Yeah. One that looks like the perfect setup to me. You're the expert on tunnels. You tell me how one of those new systems that, according to you, has been so 'expertly designed by the Serpientes,' would collapse like that." The sarcasm in his tone wasn't hard to miss.

Serpientes—Spanish for *snakes*—was the name of the new gang Dylan had been sent to Tucson to investigate. The appearance across the country of bags of heroin stamped with a distinctive red snake had sent the DEA scrambling for more info on the group based in Arizona.

The discovery of a sophisticated tunnel beneath the border at Nogales brought up a red flag. Usually tunnels dug under that border were hasty, ramshackle crawl spaces—scratched-out hollows a man could barely shimmy through. But these new tunnels were clean-cut and bolstered with supports that were strong enough for a mine. They made the transportation of drugs easy.

The violent kidnappings of two known Tucson gang members had ended in murder. All signs suggested that the Serpientes were transporting massive amounts of drugs across the border and were trying to take over the distribution of those drugs throughout the entire Southwest territory. A gang war was imminent unless the DEA could identify the leaders of the Serpientes and stop them.

The strongest link Dylan had to the Serpientes was the professionally designed tunnels, including the one where they'd found Walker. He had hoped to trace the tunnels to a qualified engineer.

Surprisingly there weren't too many of those around. He had already asked for information from mining companies, engineering organizations and schools. Hopefully they'd find a connection and maybe, just maybe, that info would lead to an explanation as to why Joss had been there.

He shook his head. "That tunnel was too well designed. It wouldn't have collapsed on its own. That's why I called in a team of experts to examine it and take some samples. It'll be a while before tests tell us if they purposely destroyed that tunnel and how. In the meantime the disappearance of Walker's brother looks suspicious."

Holmquist nodded. "Joss is close to him...really close. He's her only living relative. It doesn't make sense that he hasn't shown up after several calls and messages. We even sent a man to his apartment."

"The collapsed tunnel was discovered this morning. If Jason Walker could be here, he would."

Holmquist looked up. "What are you saying?"

Dylan focused his gaze. "You and I both know how dangerous the Serpientes are. The Mexican police chief who discovered the first tunnel had death threats sent to him. Do you think the Serpientes would be above using a family member to get what they want from a border-patrol officer?"

"You're suggesting Jason Walker could be in danger...that maybe the Serpientes have him?"

Dylan's nod was slow. "That's one possibility."

The captain gave him a sideways glance. "Another possibility is that Jason Walker is involved with the gang and dragged his sister into the middle of it. That's what you really believe, isn't it?"

Dylan didn't answer and the older man shook his head. "You've been gunning for Joss for weeks now. Why are you so sure she's involved?"

Dylan thought about the abrupt change in the woman's outgoing demeanor lately. The downward tilt of her head when they discussed the gang. The sideways glances when he tried to meet her gaze. The tense poses when she thought no one was looking. And especially her nervous habit of fingering her gun holster when she was worried. She'd been doing that a lot over the past few days.

"Let's say I recognize a person with something to hide. Joss Walker is that person. I'd stake my career on it."

Holmquist ran a hand around his neck and looked away. After a few minutes he agreed. "It's a substantial career to throw away. They don't call you the 'gang buster' for nothing."

Dylan sensed a victory and pushed home his point. "Look, I'm not saying she's guilty. I'm saying something is not right. We owe it to her to check it out. If we don't do it, someone else will. The press…other agencies…everyone is hungry for answers. They'll look at her quick advancement, at everything she's accomplished, and question her integrity. More important, they'll question your group. We owe it to her and to the rest of your officers to find the truth."

After a long while, the older man released a heavy sigh. "You're right. I don't like it, but you're right."

With that, he tossed the last of his coffee onto the ground, crushed the cup in his fingers and stalked toward the entrance, where he threw the mangled container into the trash.

Upstairs, in the waiting room, he called his employees together. "Agent Murphy has made a valid point."

Dylan ignored the virulent glares sent his way as Holmquist continued. "This looks bad for Joss. Those of us who know her know she'd never betray the department…or us. But the rest of the world doesn't. They're going to look at this situation and paint Joss dirty before she even gets out of that bed. So…" He shifted his shoulders, as if lifting a weight off, and looked around. "Instead of sitting around here like a bunch of whipped puppies, we're going to go out and do our job. Let's prove Joss innocent before the rest of the world has a chance to accuse her of being guilty."

The men and women nodded their heads. "Henderson, you've known Joss the longest. I'm sure you'd like to stay here and wait for word on her condition, but you know her best. Tomorrow I want you at her brother's apartment. Rouse the neighbors. Get some answers. I want to know where he is or when he was last seen. You know his girlfriend too, right?"

Daniel Henderson spoke up. "Maria… I do know her. I went with Joss to a birthday party for Maria's little sister, at their house."

"Good. Take Cupertino with you. Go to the mother's house. Question the girlfriend. I want to know everything I can about Walker. Evans and Hughes, go to that mechanic shop where he works. See what they know. I'm going back to the office to see about getting a warrant to search Joss's apartment. One of you needs to stay here with her."

"I'll do it," Dylan spoke up before anyone else had a chance. "I want to be here if she wakes up."

Holmquist's jaw tensed, but he worked it loose slowly. "Yeah. You're right. It might be best if someone not from the department is here when she starts to talk. That way no one can say we covered for her." That statement was aimed at Dylan. "The rest of you, go home. Get some rest. Tomorrow's going to be a busy day."

The group gathered their things and tossed their empty cups into a nearby trash can. Angry glares shot in Dylan's direction before everyone headed to the elevators.

At last he was alone. He rubbed his hands over his face and sank into a nearby chair. He'd been up since 4:00 a.m., when he'd first gotten the call. The cave-in had created a sinkhole in a cemetery on the US side of the border wall.

At one time, Dylan's team of DEA agents and the border-patrol officers had a storage building near the cemetery under surveillance. They had detected an unusual amount of traffic at the empty building and suspected it might be the cover for a tunnel. It was the perfect setup. Drugs could be delivered via the tunnel beneath the wall into the building then loaded into vehicles to be shipped out, all inside the cover of the large structure.

Unfortunately, traffic to and from the building had stopped so Dylan called a halt to the surveillance. This morning when a section of the cemetery collapsed, Dylan expedited a search warrant for the property. They found the opening of a tunnel and Walker trapped inside.

Obviously the Serpientes knew about the surveillance, realized the tunnel had been compromised and were willing to let it be destroyed for another purpose.

But what purpose was so great they were willing to lose a tunnel and five thousand dollars' worth of heroin to accomplish it? Not a small amount to a normal person, but for a group with such perfect, undetected access across the border, the heroin's value wasn't much more than chump change. Dylan suspected the Serpientes could have transported three times that. Holmquist was right. The cave-in looked like the perfect setup. But why would the gang want to incriminate Walker? What did she know that they wanted silenced?

Just one of the questions he prayed she could answer when she woke up the next time.

Dylan jerked to his feet and strode to the door, to look into her room. The nurse was finishing her hourly check on Walker's vitals. She looked up and motioned him into the room.

"Any improvement?" He kept his voice low, almost at a whisper.

"Not yet. But in situations like this, it helps to have someone the patient knows talk to them. You can touch her, hold her hand. It will help her to stabilize."

The nurse smiled and left the room. Dylan stared at Joss Walker's still form. She had a tube around her face, an IV in her arm and an oxygen monitor on her thumb. When she'd arrived, the staff had done what they could to clean her, but gray dust coated her normally black, silky hair. Still caught up with a band, her long pony-tail trailed across the white pillow. A raw, bright red scrape marked her chin.

Her free hand rested limp and lax, palm up on the bed next to Dylan. He lifted it and turned it over on his, palm to palm. She had long fingers, with nice, well-shaped nails. He'd noticed those details before. It seemed there were lots of things he'd noticed about Joss Walker.

"What happened?" he whispered. "What were you hiding? Did you find yourself trapped, like I did?"

He hadn't told Holmquist why he suspected Joss. He didn't like to remember. But now, in the silence of this room, with tubes plugged into Joss's body, he couldn't stop the memories.

An image of Rusty came to him, his best friend since they were in grade school. Hair to match his name. Fun-loving. Mischievous but never hurtful or mean. They'd stayed good friends…even when Rusty started using pills to keep him going.

At first Dylan believed his friend's claims that he could stop anytime. He just needed a little help. Needed to get that scholarship so he could go to college. After all, his parents didn't own a ranch and have money like Dylan's. Rusty had to pay his own way.

Dylan believed him…even felt guilty for his own accident of birth. He turned a blind eye to the missed assignments and dark moods. He covered for his best friend…until the day his seventeen-year-old sister Beth was found with Rusty, both of them dead from over-doses. That day had changed Dylan's life forever.

All the dropped glances and lies he'd used to hide the truth about his friend were emblazoned in his memory like white-hot embers. Those images were never far from his thoughts.

That's why he recognized the signs of deceit in Joss. He knew them well. Personally.

He looked at her unconscious body. Black dirt was caked beneath Joss's neatly shaped fingernails, evidence that she'd crawled away from the explosion. It was what saved her life. Dylan had seen the path she'd made as she'd dragged herself over the gritty gray floor of the tunnel. She must have woken in the stygian darkness, afraid, desperate…and crawled for her life.

A wave of empathy swept over him. Guilty or not, she didn't deserve that. He gripped her hand. "I'll get them. I promise. I'll make them pay."

His harsh, whispered words echoed across the silent room. He searched her face, hoping for some awareness, some movement. Nothing. Not a flicker of her eyes. Thick eyelashes lay on her cheeks. No thin, wispy lashes for this woman—they were thick and crisscrossed each other in riotous abandon. She didn't wear makeup. She didn't need it with those lashes. And eyebrows to match. Thick and dark, they defined her face, gave it character above her gray eyes. Straight nose. Slightly pointed chin. She had what Dylan supposed would be called classic features. Whatever that meant. He'd heard the expression and it seemed to fit Joss.

And that's where his wandering thoughts needed to stop. He put her hand on the bed and rubbed the bristles forming on his chin. The late hour was getting to him. He needed a break.

Dylan left the room and headed for the coffee machine. He shifted his shoulders and twisted. Hours of inactivity and lack of sleep were a potent combination… even dangerous. The last thing he needed was to imagine Joss Walker as anything other than a suspect. He couldn't lose sight of the suspicion that she was covering up for someone and had probably broken the law she'd sworn to defend.

He punched in the number for a cup of coffee and took a sip of the scalding liquid. It burned its way down his throat, searing away any lingering images. After a while he felt loose and relaxed…enough that if he sat in one of the chairs, he might fall asleep. So he stepped around the corner from the waiting room, leaned against the side of the coffee machine and slid all the way to the floor. With his knees bent up and the hot coffee in his hands, he was uncomfortable enough to stay awake. He let his head rest on the cold metal wall of the machine and closed his eyes.

Quiet slipped over the waiting room. The silence helped him think. Where was Jason Walker? Dylan was almost 100 percent certain that's who Joss was protecting. Everyone knew she was close to her brother. Dylan had known her for a little over a month, and he knew the details of her past. Joss wasn't secretive. They'd discussed many things, including how she hated monsoon season. Her father, the owner of a corner convenience store, had been killed in a robbery gone haywire right after a massive storm.

Joss's mother ran the store and took care of her kids until she contracted a rare kidney disease and passed away when Joss was still in high school.

Jason Walker left college to take care of his sister and the family business, but it was too much for him. He lost the store and started to work as a mechanic, at the shop where he was still employed. Joss went on to college, graduated with honors and entered the academy, where she finished at the top of her class. She'd often spoken to Dylan about the sacrifices her brother had made and how much she owed her good life to him. When she talked about it, she almost sounded guilty... an emotion Dylan understood only too well.

It seemed her father's tragic death had charted her path, much as his sister's death had set Dylan on his course. They had that much in common. Did they also share the need to protect someone they cared about?

The click of a door opening interrupted Dylan's stream of thought. Probably the nurse taking Joss's vitals again. He closed his eyes. But when he didn't hear the corresponding click of the door closing, it puzzled him. Peeking around the corner, he saw a man dressed in medical scrubs—but he'd come from the door leading to the stairs, not the nurse's station, which was in the opposite direction. He'd held the door in a stealthy manner so it would not click shut. His head was shaved, and tattoos covered one arm and crawled up his neck. Dylan couldn't see what they were. Something else caught his attention. The man carried a syringe in one hand. His efforts at silence and his furtive movements struck an alarm bell.

The man paused to look around. Dylan ducked behind the machine. He wanted to know where the guy was headed before he acted. After a few moments he looked out again. The man was headed straight for Joss's door.

Dylan dropped his empty cup and lunged to his feet. He moved quietly so the man wouldn't see him coming, but Dylan would never be able to stop him from entering Joss's room in time. The man was too far ahead of him. He had to do something.

"Hey!" His shout rang through the halls of the sleeping hospital. "What are you doing?"

The man halted. Seeing Dylan running toward him, he spun and ran for the stairs. Dylan dashed across the space, to catch him at the portal. Just as Dylan reached for him, the man spun around, slashing crosswise with the hypodermic needle. Dylan dodged, hit the chairs behind him and tumbled over. He landed hard and was momentarily stunned. By the time he got to his feet, the man was out the door and gone.

Torn between giving chase and staying by Joss's side, he hesitated. A nurse came running up. "What's going on?"

"Someone tried to get into Joss's room. Stay with her!"

He dashed down the stairs, pausing at each floor. At the bottom, he ran into the hall. A security guard was looking out the window by the exit. Dylan moved toward him, holding out his badge. The guard straightened.

"Did a man with a shaved head come by here?"

"Yeah, just jumped into a truck and drove away."

"Did you see the license plate?"

"No, but I got a good look at the truck. Older Toyota. Four-wheel drive with the tow bar. Gunmetal gray. Seen better days."

"Would you recognize the man if you saw him again?"

"Maybe. Caught my attention, since he seemed in a hurry. Walked outta here pretty fast."

"Call the Tucson police. I think he might have tried to kill a patient."

The guard hurried to his desk and picked up the

phone. Dylan pulled out his cell and dialed Holmquist's number. The officer answered on the second ring.

"I'm sorry to say we're going to be dealing with another agency sooner than either of us wanted. I told hospital security to call the police. I'm going to arrange twenty-four-hour protection for Walker. I think the Serpientes just sent a man to kill her."

TWO

Dylan strode down the hospital hallway and nodded toward the nurses at their station. He was getting to be a familiar face here. Five days, and Joss still swam in pain and memory loss. He'd barely left her side, but there'd been no break in her pain, no flashes of recollection.

He was starting to worry. Every day the Serpientes grew stronger. Another body had been discovered in the desert, executed. The victim was another known gang member, but why he was executed and how he was connected to the Serpientes remained a mystery.

The group was so new and close-knit, he had not yet found anyone willing to inform on them. But they were making enemies with the rival gang, and some of those members were beginning to talk. Information had begun to filter in, and Dylan had taken the time to meet with his agents. That meant precious time away from Joss.

Holmquist stood outside her door, chatting with the guard. The supervisor gestured to the closed portal. "Her doctor's in there now."

"I see." Dylan nodded. "Any change?"

Holmquist scuffed a foot in a frustrated gesture and shook his head. "Not a one. She's asking for you though."

Dylan tensed. Everyone had noticed and remarked on Joss's growing attachment to him. She asked for him continually and seemed agitated when he was gone. "I was the first person she saw when she woke. I'm her only familiar face. That's all."

The captain stepped closer, away from the guard so only Dylan could hear. "Yeah. She trusts you. But I gotta wonder what you're gonna do when she finds out you think she's guilty."

Dylan met the man's level stare. "By that time her memory will have returned and it won't matter what I think. Right now I want her to be as comfortable and relaxed as possible."

Holmquist worked his jaw, a habit that showed his frustration. "Right. So you can solve your case. That's all that matters, right?"

"That's all that should matter to you too. The Serpientes are vicious and Joss could be their next victim. That's more important than how she feels about me."

"There's more than one way to be a victim, Murphy." His tone was stone cold. "Joss has been through enough. I don't want to see her hurt more."

Dylan met his gaze. "Trust me. Nothing hurts worse than knowing people are dead because of you."

Joss's supervisor studied him, but Dylan said no more. Finally the man turned away. "This case is going nowhere. We have no new leads and it's not even in my jurisdiction. We will have to return to our regular duties monitoring the border checkpoints like nothing ever happened. It'll be turned over to the police now that they're involved."

"And me."

Holmquist twisted his neck from side to side as if it hurt. "And you." The words seemed to leave him with a sour taste.

"You'll be happy to know you're still on the case. I just got word this morning. I've been given permission to expand the task force to include most of your unit. I need all the help I can get."

"With you as the lead?"

Dylan nodded.

Holmquist looked away. "I don't like your tactics, Murphy. You're a driven man. But I guess you're the one for the job. The sooner we get these creeps, the sooner Joss will be safe…from all of you."

"You have my word, sir. Joss is safe with me. I intend to keep her comfortable while she regains her memory. Things between us won't go any further than that."

Holmquist studied Dylan. "I think you're driven enough to keep that promise."

Dylan tried not to flinch. He'd never thought of himself as driven. Strong-willed. Purposeful and successful. But not driven. Especially not so driven as to take advantage of Joss's emotional state. No matter what Holmquist thought.

"Well, *lead* agent, I hope you have somewhere to go, because we've hit a dead end. Joss's brother hasn't shown up for work since the day before the cave-in. And what's more, Maria Martinez, Walker's girlfriend, and her family have disappeared. No one's at home and the little sister hasn't been to school."

"We're not at a dead end yet. One of my agents here in Tucson found a contact who's talking. We have a name for their leader. Vibora."

Holmquist shook his head. "Viper. Sounds about right for this guy. He's crazy."

"I've got my home office searching records for any connections to the name Vibora. If we can find a real name associated with that gang tag, we'll have our first lead. See if you can expedite a search warrant for Walker's apartment and the Martinez home." He paused. "You should be happy. We didn't find anything in Joss's apartment."

"Nope. It was clean as a whistle."

"Well then, Joss is in the clear. You should be relieved."

"I would be if any other special agent was in charge."

Dylan smiled. "I think you just paid me a compliment."

Holmquist returned a tight little smile before he turned and walked away. "Don't let it go to your head, Murphy."

"Are you telling me I might never regain my memory?" Joss held her breath. Doctor Hull avoided meeting her gaze by studying the computer screen on the cart by her bed.

"I'm saying it's too soon to tell. Physically you are doing phenomenally well. Most people with a concussion as severe as yours would still be struggling to sit up. You were in excellent condition before your…accident."

Joss's jaw tightened. "That's what they tell me. I, of course, don't remember."

The doctor's eyebrows rose and he looked at her over the screen. "You'd think after what you've been through you would be willing to give yourself time to rest."

She took a deep, tight breath. "If I knew what I'd been through, maybe I would. But right now all I want is to remember. I want my life back."

"You still have no recollection of the accident or anything leading up to it?"

Joss closed her eyes and rested on the pillow. She willed her racing mind to be calm, to think…to remember. All she could see was a gray wall behind her closed eyes. Her jaw tightened and she looked at the older man.

"Nothing. Absolutely nothing. Just this irritating feeling that something is about to happen. I need to remember… I need to…" She sighed. "I need to stop something. But I don't know how or even what it is."

He pulled a pen light out of his coat pocket and kept up the conversation while he examined her pupils. "Maybe if you stop putting so much pressure on yourself, things will come back to you."

"Someone tried to kill me. There's a guard outside my hospital room and border-patrol officers hover around me 24/7. I don't think I'm the one putting pressure on myself."

He paused. "Are they bothering you? If you want me to ban them from your room, I will."

She shook her head and the little movement brought

on a twinge of vertigo. She closed her eyes, letting the moment of dizziness pass before she spoke again. "No. They're trying to protect my feelings, so they won't answer my questions. But that doesn't help me when I know someone is trying to kill me. Or that I was found in a tunnel beneath the border, with a cache of drugs. They all seem to think I'm innocent, but…"

Dr. Hull waited, not rushing or pushing for a response. That, more than anything, gave her the courage to say what she really felt. "No matter how kind they are, that sounds guilty to me."

"Is that how you feel—guilty?" He turned her head to the side, gently examining the bruise and swelling at the base of her skull.

Did she feel guilty? So many emotions swirled inside of her. Confusion. Anger. Fear. Mostly fear…of the unknown…of men she couldn't remember trying to kill her. And now fear of not ever remembering. Of disappointing all of those very nice people outside her room.

They all seemed to care so much about her, and she couldn't remember their names. As kind as they were, they seemed to want…*need* confirmation from her that she was innocent. Confirmation she couldn't give them.

The only one who didn't make her feel that way was Dylan. He didn't seem to have expectations. At least not the same hopeful kind she sensed in everyone else. He made her feel like the truth was as important to him as it was to her.

The doctor's gentle fingers touched a particularly tender spot and she winced.

"Still pretty sore there, I take it."

She looked up to meet his gaze. "They all know so much about me and I know nothing."

"You need to give yourself a break. You had a serious head injury and you've only been cognizant for a short while. Besides you know more than you think."

"Like what?"

"Well, you know you heal quickly."

She directed a frown in his direction.

"I'm not just placating you. Think about what you know instead of what you don't. You're very healthy and strong-willed. That's apparent."

That comment made a small wry twist slide over her lips. "I take it I haven't been the best patient."

The doctor's lips lifted. "You're impatient and you have a strong sense of right and wrong. Most people aren't so willing to admit they might be guilty."

That was the truth. She expelled her breath, slow and easy. Some of the taut, tense fear flowed out with it.

"As your doctor, I order you to stop fixating on what you don't know and start rediscovering yourself. You'll find more answers there than in your determination to remember what happened."

"But something's wrong. It needs to be stopped. I know it. I can feel it."

"Probably. But if your friends are doing their jobs, they'll find the answers without your help. In the meantime, you concentrate on you. On what makes you feel good and relaxed. Stop beating yourself up. Someone else already did that for you."

Joss relaxed her shoulders and tried to ignore the

tight band across her stomach. "I know one thing. You're a pretty good doctor."

He gave her a nod. "Remember that when you get my bill." He patted her leg through the blanket. "I'll see you later today to sign your release papers. You're going home."

Home. Where was that? An apartment or a house? What did it look like? Comfy? Or bare essentials? Did she like to cook, or was she more of a takeout person? Did she have a pet? Was something warm and furry waiting for her? If so, did someone think to take care of it while she was in the hospital?

Wait! Did she have a boyfriend? No. Surely not. If she did he would have been in to see her, right? All of Dr. Hull's orders flew out the window as panic built inside her. She didn't even know what she liked to eat!

The door opened and Dylan eased into the room. His curly hair looked slightly mussed, and the shadow of a beard graced his jawline. Instead of appearing scruffy, he seemed warm and welcoming, like he was ready for an afternoon on the couch. Joss couldn't believe how much the idea appealed to her. Sitting beside him, watching football, with tons of cheese puffs and potato chips.

Okay. She liked football. Cheese puffs. Potato chips. And Dylan. And not necessarily in that order.

Dr. Hull was right. Concentrating on what she knew, instead of what she didn't, helped. But there were two things she couldn't forget, no matter how hard she tried. People were trying to kill her. So was home a safe place?

Second, she had to go, safe or not. She needed to

trigger her memory, because something bad was going to happen if she didn't stop it. Time was slipping away and she had to do something!

Groaning, she covered her face with her hands.

"Did the doctor give you bad news?"

The sound of Dylan's voice, deep and resonant, somewhat eased the tight ball of fear in her stomach. His voice was the only thing she remembered...that and his singing. He had a habit of humming old hymns. She'd fallen asleep and woken many times to the sound of his low-key tones. She remembered some of the lyrics clearly. They came through strong, piercing the haze of pain. They were about the only things she did remember from the past few days. Those songs and his voice brought her comfort. With all the anxiety flowing through her, she needed that comfort more than anything right now.

A small smile slipped out... She couldn't stop it. She was that relieved to see him.

"That depends."

"On what?"

"On how you and Holmquist feel. Dr. Hull says he'll be releasing me today."

"That's good news. Why does that make you unhappy?"

She hesitated. "You'll have to make special arrangements, send more personnel to watch over me and..."

"Stop right there. You are not to think about those details. Let us do the worrying."

Easier said than done. But with him, it worked. That calm reassurance went deep. How did he do it? What was it about him that eased the terror threatening to eat her alive?

That sense of safety with Dylan helped her go a step further and admit the truth. "I—I don't know what I'm going home to."

His eyebrows rose in a quizzical gesture. "You're right. That is something to worry about. I don't know how I'd feel either. Am I a neat freak? Do I hang my clothes or drop them? Am I a toilet paper up or down fellow?"

Joss giggled and a sharp pain shot through her temples. She stilled instantly, but couldn't stop a little chuckle. "Don't make me laugh. It hurts."

"Okay. But seriously. I can't help you there. I don't know what your place looks like."

"No? I thought you said we were friends."

"Not that kind. We're friends and we got along well. We've only known each other since I was transferred here to be the special agent on this case. About a month. We hadn't graduated to visiting each other's places, but we have common beliefs. We're both Christians. You understood when I said my work was more of a call-ing…a God-given mission."

That's why the words to his songs comforted her so much. She was a Christian. She knew the songs. They meant something to her. It made sense. But what made more sense was the voice singing them. Dylan was reli-able, strong in his faith but most of all safe. She sensed that now, even when she couldn't remember anything else about her life.

Oblivious to where her thoughts had led her, Dylan continued. "We work well together."

That gave her pause. "How?"

Her interruption threw him off. "What do you mean?"

"How do we work well together? Holmquist tells me you're called the 'gang buster.' What do I do that helps you?"

He hesitated. "I think... I think we have the same goal...to protect people. That's very important to me."

"Why?"

Again he let the question lie while he thought about it. Was he trying to decide how much to tell her, or was he hesitating because he was going to tell her something personal about his own life? She hoped it was personal. She wanted to know more about him. Wanted to understand her deep-seated attraction to him.

He'd been her near-constant companion since she had awakened. He made her feel safe and protected. But she sensed her feelings went deeper. Had she been attracted to him before her accident? She needed to know, to understand something about her past and especially about him.

"I had a sister. Her name was Beth." His voice dropped when he said her name. Almost as if he couldn't speak the name out loud. Joss tensed. Whatever he was about to tell her pained him a great deal.

"She was my little sister, two years younger than me. She was beautiful and bright. Long dark hair...like yours. Only, hers was curly like mine." A smile flashed across his lips. Gone in a moment. "She followed me everywhere…even in high school. That's why I should have seen it. I should have realized."

He shook his head. The pain in his expression went so deep, it hurt to see it. Reaching out, she grasped his hand. His touch was familiar. It had been like an anchor these past few days, keeping her from flying into empty space, from losing herself in darkness. She hoped she could do the same for him.

"Don't. Don't say more. I'm sorry I asked."

He shook his head and gripped her hand, met her gaze. "It's important, Joss. I want you to know."

There was more…so much more behind the words. Something he wasn't saying. But his hand was warm and strong. She wanted to bring it to her lips and kiss it, to thank him for trusting her.

But that would make him uncomfortable. Her emotions were too strong and overwhelming for the casual relationship he'd described. He'd told her they were friends. They clicked and worked well together. His words exactly. But Joss had the feeling "clicked" had meant a lot more to her, something Dylan didn't want to acknowledge or discuss. Every time she'd tried to express her gratitude, to explain the unusual bond she felt with him, he grew uncomfortable and changed the subject. So she held her feelings and the words back.

"All right." If she couldn't comfort him in the way she wanted to, she could at least give him permission to share his heartache. "Tell me."

He swallowed. "I went off to college and left Beth behind. Two years later she was dead from an overdose. She was seventeen."

Joss was silent for a long while, as she searched for words. "I'm sorry. So sorry. But it wasn't your fault... you were young."

He gripped her hand with both of his and looked deep into her eyes. "But that's the problem, Joss. It was my fault. I could have stopped it. She had a crush on my best friend, Rusty. He got her involved in the drug scene. I knew he was hooked on painkillers long before Beth started hanging out with him. I turned a blind eye to his usage, Joss. I covered up for him. I could have told his parents...told mine. They would never have trusted him with Beth. But they knew he was my best friend, thought he'd never let anything happen to her..."

His words trailed off into excruciating silence. Anger twisted his features. Anger and frustration...pain so strong, Joss could barely stand it.

She didn't know what to say, didn't understand the significance of why it was important for her to know. She only understood how it had impacted his life. "That's why you say your work is a God-given mission."

He nodded, never loosening his grip on her hand. "I stood over her coffin, stared at her emaciated body—I barely recognized my beautiful, vibrant little sister. My parents told me she was having problems. They thought it was an eating disorder, maybe depression. They didn't suspect drugs and I didn't want to believe Rusty would betray me like that...not until the evidence lay in front of me. I promised God right there and then that I would devote my life to stopping drug traffickers."

She gripped his hand. "You've done it, Dylan. Holmquist tells me you have one of the best records of success in the DEA. That's why they sent you here. You can be at ease. You've honored your promise."

"More than a promise, Joss. A vow, and it was my duty." He lifted her hand, squeezing tighter. "My sister died because I covered for my friend Rusty. I was responsible."

His intense gaze made her uncomfortable. "What are you trying to tell me, Dylan? Is there something I should know?"

The tension in his body eased and he released her hand. "No. No. I'm just... I don't talk about Beth much. Not ever, really. I guess I got carried away."

She smiled. "Thank you...for sharing. It means a lot to me."

He looked away and shifted. "You need to stop thanking me so much. I'm only doing what needs to be done. And besides." He gave her a sheepish grin. "We don't usually talk about serious stuff. I call you 'hot shot.' You call me 'special.' We argue over football teams. Mine, of course, is better."

So they did share football! She'd gotten something right. They also had common beliefs, as well as faith and confidence in the justice system. Maybe Dr. Hull knew what he was talking about. All she needed to do was to concentrate on what she did know. That was easier to do around Dylan, because for her, he *was* special.

Swallowing her fear, she said, "Which is my team?"

A sly twist slipped over his lips. "Well...how will you know I'm telling the truth? Maybe I'll make you a Wildcat so when your memory comes back, you'll remember the Sun Devils and know I got you."

The attempted joke didn't work, mainly because it reminded her that she might not ever remember. That made her future a big black hole, just like her past. She turned to him, all humor gone. "I trust you. You're the only one I can trust right now."

The wry twist faded and he looked away. "You know, I'm going to try to catch Holmquist before he leaves."

The door closed behind him and the room seemed empty. In spite of what he had said, her release from the hospital was going to be a tactical nightmare. The city police would have to schedule someone to watch over her 24/7. Maybe her friends—the friends she couldn't remember—would have to volunteer their time to guard her. The extra expense and stress would be ridiculous. Who would pay for it? How long could it last?

And…those men were still out there…trying to kill her. Why? Was that the terrible thing she needed to prevent? Her own murder? That was a horrifying thought.

She was letting the deep dark holes overwhelm her again. She tried to slow the raging questions exploding in her mind.

If Dylan would just come back. He was so strong and vital. His presence filled a room…drove out the dark holes. She could wrap his vitality around her like a warm, safe blanket and she needed that…needed something or she might tip over the edge.

As if on cue, the door opened and he returned. A slight smile tilted his lips. "Holmquist is staying. He wants to be here when you check out." He seemed relieved.

She said nothing. Her supervisor's concern was nice

but she really wanted Dylan there. "You're coming with me, right?"

"Of course. Wouldn't miss your return home."

An undertone of intensity laced his lightly stated words and gave her pause. "Why?"

He frowned. "Because we need to answer the all-important question. Do you throw clothes in a corner or hang them neatly in the closet?"

Caught off guard, she let another small chortle slip out. "*Owww.* I told you not to make me laugh."

"Can't help it. I'm dying to find out your dark secrets." His words held an undertone of…something. A sincerity that took her by surprise. She stared at him.

He lifted his gaze upward, clearly striving for a deep-in-thought expression "I'm pretty sure you are a 'hang it very neatly' type."

He meant to make her laugh, but she sensed something behind his words. What was it? Was she an unpleasant, uptight woman he didn't like?

"You make me sound like a prude. Am I?"

He stopped to consider. "No. Thorough. By the book. Sincere. Passionate about your work. But easy to be around. Energetic and full of questions. Fun. You're surrounded by friends all of the time. You told me once you don't like to be alone…ever." He started to say more but halted and clammed up. A strange look came over his features…a look she couldn't define. Was he holding something back? Picking and choosing what to tell her about herself?

When he said no more, she released a sigh. "Maybe

I'm someone I'd like if I knew me." Her tone sounded more forlorn than she'd intended.

"Everyone likes you, Joss. You're a good agent and a great person."

Shaking her head, she met his gaze. "If I'm such a good agent, what was I doing in that tunnel with a payload of illegal drugs?"

Dylan was saved from answering when Holmquist walked in. Surprised at how relieved he was, he stepped away and turned to stare out the window.

Finding out why Joss was in that tunnel was the reason he was here, spending every free moment with her rather than pounding the street, searching for answers. Yes, his team of agents was on the job, and they were making breakthroughs. But he should be with them. Yet when she posed the question…gave him the perfect opportunity to start probing for answers…he backed off. Hesitated. What was wrong with him?

Holmquist reviewed the details of Joss's release with her. She asked a few questions, a thread of fear running behind every word. She was scared and barely hanging on. That was the reason he'd stopped probing. Because he hadn't wanted to push her into that dark hole.

But why was he hesitating now…almost feeling guilty? He glanced at Joss. In some ways she reminded him of Beth. Not so much in looks, even though they both had dark hair. But more in personality. Beth had been bright, outgoing and fun, but a thread of insecurity had run deep, pushed her in the wrong directions.

She'd hungered for approval…for support from others, including Rusty. That need had led to her death.

Dylan sensed the same longing in Joss. She'd always seemed competent, sure of her work, but he'd sensed an underlying need to belong, not to be alone. And now that underlying need had come to the surface. She was completely vulnerable. Now was the time to push for answers, not to ease up.

He needed to get on course, to break those fears loose so they could get to the truth…for both their sakes. "While we wait, let me bring you up to speed." He addressed his comments to Holmquist. "We have an initial report about those traces of chemicals we found on the support post in the mine. They definitely come from some sort of explosive. They don't know the type yet."

"Explosives." Joss shook her head. "In the mine? What does that mean?"

Holmquist shot a puzzled glance in Dylan's direction, obviously wondering why he was discussing details of the investigation in front of Joss while she was in her fragile state. But Dylan ignored him.

"It means the cave-in was deliberately set."

Her features brightened. "Does that prove they were trying to kill me? That I'm innocent?"

Dylan shook his head. "Unfortunately no. The explosion could have been a cover-up. You could have set the explosion and been trapped."

Now Holmquist gave him an angry frown. But Dylan ignored it. Joss was almost as passionate about her work as he was. Or at least she had seemed to be…and that was what he needed to determine. Now that she was vulnerable, the truth might come out. Had her loyalty been an act? Was she good at making them all like her? Was that her true motivation—the need to be liked, not the desire to stop crime? If that was true, she was just like his sister, and that weakness could have turned Joss away from a righteous path. She might care more about the people she loved than the law, and that love could have led her into that tunnel.

Now, with no recollection of her past, the real woman beneath the facade would come to light. With no memory to protect her, the next days would reveal Joss's guilt…or innocence.

With his resolve renewed, he faced Holmquist. "Also, my home office can find nothing on Vibora. Nothing."

"Vibora?"

Both men turned to Joss as her brow furrowed.

Dylan paused. "What? Do you remember something?"

Her frown deepened, almost as if it hurt to think. After a long while she shook her head. "No. Nothing. But I know what it means. Viper. Do I speak Spanish?"

She looked at Holmquist, and her expression was so full of hope, it almost hurt to see it.

He shook his head. "Just enough to get by."

The beginnings of a smile flitted over her lips. "Then I remember it. The name means something to me."

She looked happy that she had one memory. She didn't realize that already knowing the leader's gang name, when all of them had just discovered it, implicated her.

Holmquist looked at Dylan, his features grim and

angry. Dylan looked away. The truth was the ultimate goal…no matter how much Holmquist didn't want to hear it.

The captain's radio crackled to life.

"We've got an intruder matching the description of the attacker. He's on the fourth floor, headed toward the stairs."

Joss's room was on the fifth floor. Holmquist's gaze darted to Dylan. Dylan was younger, faster and probably stronger. Holmquist gave Dylan a sharp nod and he dashed out the door.

As it closed behind him, Joss cried out. "Wait! Don't go!"

Her desperate tone sent a sharp pain through him, but he pushed it aside and turned to the guard outside. "You heard the report?"

The man nodded.

"Holmquist is inside. Whatever happens, don't leave this door unguarded."

Another nod. Dylan strode down the hall and raised his voice. "Everyone clear this hall."

He shut the door of the room closest to him and went on to the next. A nurse pushing a cart full of medications paused.

He gestured to the nearest room. "Go on. Step inside and close the door."

A man in a hospital gown pushed an IV stand on its wheels. He turned and headed to his room. "That's too far. Go in here."

Dylan guided the patient to the nearest room and closed the door.

The hall was empty. He unlatched his gun from its holster and released the lock. Directly in front of him, the elevator lay at the junction of the T-shaped hall. The door to the stairwell was around the corner...out of his vision. He moved forward, settled against the wall and peeked around the corner. The hall was empty. The intruder had not yet reached this floor.

Dylan waited, gun drawn. Hands bracing the gun, wrists taut. Nothing happened.

Should he move closer to the storage room on the right? Wait inside, then pop out and get behind the intruder?

No. Better to keep himself between the man and Joss.

He heard a noise in the stairwell. Heavy footfalls echoed from behind the door. The intruder was close. Dylan gripped the gun. At that moment the elevator dinged. The doors slid open. A man, his wife and two laughing children prepared to step out.

"Get back! Stay inside!"

The frightened father pulled the children to him and pushed his wife inside. The mother frantically jabbed at the elevator buttons. Dylan turned to see the stairway door slowly closing.

Groaning his frustration, he ran toward it. Carefully he pulled it open and waited for gunfire. Nothing happened, so he peeked out. The man was gone. Stepping inside the echoing stairwell, he could hear footsteps— so many, it was hard to distinguish where they were coming from. He paused, listening, and heard the low instructions of the police as they systematically moved up the stairwell together.

Then he heard steps above him. He shouted, "This is Agent Murphy. He's headed to the sixth floor."

No men were stationed on the sixth floor. Three officers were stationed below him, plus the guard at Joss's door. Dylan was ahead of everyone. If the intruder were to be caught, he'd have to do it himself.

He took the steps two at a time, reaching the sixth floor just as the door shut. He flung it open and waited. No shots were fired. He moved into the hall in time to see another set of elevator doors close and the lights above flash on. This was the surgery level and, the elevator was strictly for service. It didn't open onto the other floors, but went straight to the basement.

Spinning, Dylan took the stairs two at a time, shouting again. "He's on the service elevator, headed for the basement. I don't have a radio. Call security and have them send someone there." He met the three policemen coming up and they all headed down.

One of the policemen's radios crackled, but no one responded. "I'm not getting any reception in the stairwell."

Dylan stifled his frustration and they descended to the bottom, coming out in the brightly lit, wide-open basement. The entrance to the laundry room on the right. On the left, a massive generator. Other doors led to other rooms. Too many rooms. Too many nooks and crannies in which to hide.

One of the policemen gestured across the room. "Look."

Yet another door at the far end was closing. A bright shaft of sunlight slashed across metal steps before it closed. Dylan raced across the room, with the other men close behind. They lunged out the door in time to see a gray Toyota truck screech away through the alley.

The guard had seen the same truck speeding away the first time the gang had tried to reach Joss. This time Dylan was close enough to see the license plate, but a coating of strategically placed mud made it indecipherable.

Clever. No traffic cop would stop them for a blob of mud, but at the same time, no one could track them. The Serpientes were cunning, deceptive and incredibly bold to attack Joss twice while she was under protection.

What did they want from her? What did Joss know that they were so desperate to silence?

THREE

Joss shifted in the hospital chair. It squeaked, a sound that grated against her nerves. She'd sat here for almost forty minutes. Dressed and ready to go. Waiting. And waiting. Holmquist had demanded a thorough search of each floor of the hospital before he would agree to let her leave.

After the latest scare and Dylan's recognition of the familiar Toyota truck, Holmquist had insisted she stay one more night at the hospital. In all honesty, Joss hadn't minded the extra night of service in bed. The staff had stopped monitoring her vitals, so it had been a relatively peaceful night…probably the last for a few nights to come. Because frankly, going home wouldn't be the relief everyone thought. Holmquist said it would be nice to be in her own bed again, right? Dylan commented on how she would feel better surrounded by her own things.

They were both wrong. Going home had taken on the epic proportions of a nightmare because she couldn't remember a thing about it…not her bed, nor a single solitary possession. She didn't even recognize the sweats Dylan had brought for her. Were they from her closet or the store?

She didn't know and the whole idea of going home frightened her. What if this long-awaited moment came and nothing jogged her memory? What if nothing looked familiar? Worse…what if she opened her closet and didn't like anything she saw inside?

The thick gray wall in her mind, the one she'd encountered when she first opened her eyes, remained in place—thicker than ever. As the time passed and the person on the other side of the gray mist—the pre-explosion Jocelyn—moved farther and farther away. Dr. Hull had told her to focus on what she knew, and she had diligently worked at that. The problem was, the harder she tried, the less she liked the woman Dylan described.

Easygoing. Ummm…not. She was wound about as tightly, and just about as fearfully, as a person could get.

Fun. Well, she might crack a smile if she could find something to smile about. No. That wasn't true. Dylan made her happy. He was the only bright spot in all of this.

He said she was a good agent. Right. So, why had she been alone, out of uniform, in a tunnel full of thousands of dollars' worth of heroin?

No matter how many different questions she asked herself, she always circled back to that one. And that was where she hit the blank wall of gray mist with nothing behind it. Nothing.

She sighed. The chair creaked and she cringed. Her

head ached. Soon it would be pounding. She was weak. Her legs felt like wet noodles. If they didn't hurry up with this inspection, someone might have to carry her into her apartment.

A vision of Dylan lifting her in his arms popped into her mind. He gave off a sense of whipcord strength. He wouldn't have trouble lifting her. How would he smell? Aftershave or not?

Wait. How much did a bulletproof vest weigh? The bulky apparel wrapped around her torso felt pretty heavy to her. Coupled with her own weight...

How much did she weigh? How tall was she? She'd glanced in the mirror during one of her trips to the bathroom, and the woman staring at her didn't look familiar, just tall and gangly and too heavy to carry.

Okay. So being carried into her place was not a good idea. She groaned and covered her face with her hands.

People were trying to kill her. Guards stood outside her room and throughout the building to protect her. She had a ticking time bomb in her head, warning of some impending danger, and here she sat, worrying about her weight.

Some kind of agent she was.

The more she knew about herself, the more nothing fit together. She wasn't the person she had been...the good and sturdy agent everyone liked. Would she ever be that person again?

The door flew open and she jerked.

"Sorry, I didn't mean to startle you."

Dylan's voice rolled across her jangled nerves. That voice. Deep and smooth. Coming out of the darkness.

The only thing that still felt familiar and safe. She released a small sigh of relief.

"Are you all right? You look a little pale. Do you need some help?"

Absolutely not. No lifting or carrying. No contact. "No. I'm fine." She lunged to her feet.

Too fast. Too soon. The world spun in a dangerous whirlwind and she tilted. Before she knew it, an arm snaked around her waist and held her still.

Whipcord strong. Stable. Safe. Silly or not, she leaned into his shoulder and rested, waiting for the world to right itself again.

Dylan only meant to catch her, to keep her from falling, but the minute his arm went around her waist, something happened. She felt slender and so fragile. He could wrap his arm completely around her even with the bulky bulletproof vest. He already knew how fragile her mental state was, but to feel her slight, wispy frame sent a wave of protectiveness washing over him.

She was terrified and trying so hard to be brave and strong. He grasped her tighter and turned her body slightly inward. Her head slipped perfectly into the crook of his neck and he held her there. Safe. Protected.

I won't let them get to you, Joss. Not like they got to Beth...at least not until you remember.

That was what he was here for, right? To keep her calm and stable so she could remember. That was all. With that thought, he placed his other hand on the curve of her waist and gently pulled her away. Her head was wobbly and her gaze a bit unfocused. He ducked to look into her eyes. The sight of those gray eyes, so wide and lost, almost undid him. He wanted to pull her into his arms and keep her there.

Resisting the urge, he guided her toward the chair. "Maybe you better sit."

She shook her head and clung to him. "If I go down again, I might not get up. Just give me a minute." She tucked her head into the crook of his neck. A jolt of pure, white-hot need to protect shot through him.

Holding her safe in his arms felt so right. It wouldn't hurt to let her stay there a little longer.

The door burst open and Holmquist stepped inside. "We're ready—"

His gaze hardened as he stared at Joss.

Dylan gritted his teeth and tried not to look guilty. "Can you get the wheelchair? I think she's going to pass out." Did his words sound as lame as he thought?

Thankfully Joss lifted her head from his shoulder. "No…no. I'm all right. I just felt a little woozy. Really, I'm fine now."

"You're going to sit in the wheelchair. The hospital won't let you leave without it." Dylan tried to sound firm, not to let a twinge of regret echo in his tone. Was he really that sorry she was leaving his arms? If that were true, he was in dangerous territory. Joss was suspect in his mind. He couldn't afford to be swayed by his attraction…or her need. Finding the truth was all that mattered.

The aide came in the door with the chair. Dylan eased Joss into it and the young woman adjusted the footrests. As she took the handles and pushed toward the door, Holmquist grasped Dylan's arm and held him back.

As soon as Joss was out the door, Dylan turned to face the older man. "Look, I'm not comfortable with the fact that she's becoming so attached to me. But what can I do about it? She needs something familiar to hang onto and that seems to be me."

Holmquist's gaze narrowed. "She can hang onto you for now. I'm just making sure you don't do the same. I know you think she's guilty. What kind of a mess will you be creating if this—" he circled his finger around the room "—thing between you two continues?"

"What do you want me to do? Tell her I think she was involved with the gang? She already doubts herself and questions why she was in that tunnel. I need to push, but I'm not going to shove her over the edge."

Holmquist hooked his thumbs in his gun belt. "Somehow that doesn't make me feel better. You want her to convict herself."

"I want the truth, Holmquist. You should too."

The man looked away and shook his head. "Oh, I do. And I'm convinced the truth will prove Joss innocent. What I'm concerned about is getting my agent back when all this is said and done. I don't want her broken so badly she can't return."

"And you think I'll be responsible for 'breaking' her?"

"You tell me, Murphy. Her brother's missing…maybe dead. Some kind of spark obviously exists between you two. It was there before the cave-in."

Dylan was surprised. He wouldn't have called it a

spark. He didn't allow "sparks" in his life. Only level-headed relationships where they both knew his work came first. He and Joss had a connection, sure, that was obvious. He was attracted to her. But he'd stomped on those feelings when he had begun to suspect she was covering up something.

"You're the only person in the world she trusts right now. She doesn't even trust herself, and you're determined to prove she's guilty. What should I think?"

He opened his mouth to reassure Holmquist…and then paused. His reaction to Joss moments ago had shaken his conviction. To deny something unusual had happened would be a lie. He had overstepped his own line. Had he already gone too far? Was he on a path of no return?

He released a slow breath. "Let's hope going home will trigger her memory so we can find the answers we all need."

Joss's head was beginning to throb. Even with the vehicle's air-conditioning blasting, she was hot and sweaty. Moving fifty miles an hour down the street, in a police car, caused the sights to blur when she tried to focus.

Small, beige pueblo-style houses with dirt yards looked like they'd been built in the fifties. Miracle Mile with its fifties-style motor hotels, wide-open courts and old-fashioned fluorescent signs. Slowly they gave way to strip malls. Nicer restaurants. Tall palm trees waved in the air, and squat ones grew in pointy clumps. Saguaros with their lifelike arms pointing up in the air.

Oleanders bloomed with white, red and purple flowers. Five lanes of black asphalt wound straight ahead, far into the cloud-filled skies. Dark gray, the puffy billows tumbled over each other, threatening rain.

August in Tucson. Monsoon season. Storms rumbled up from the Gulf of California. She could remember the historical district of Miracle Mile and monsoons, but not one single thing about herself. She couldn't recall the most important aspects of her own life. They'd disappeared into the gray mist.

Thunder boomed and she jumped.

"You okay?" Dylan sat beside her.

"I don't like storms."

"Do you know why?"

She shook her head. Another thing she didn't remember.

Thunder rumbled again and she gripped Dylan's hand.

He lowered his voice. "Are you sure you're all right?"

The sky emptied. Rain poured down in buckets and fell on the street so hard, it bounced. Great sheets of blinding water slid off the windshield.

"Whoa." The driver of the cruiser slowed almost to a crawl. Up ahead, a streetlight turned from red to green. The driver accelerated ever so slowly. Out of the corner of her eye, Joss caught movement and looked up. A car was speeding toward them, so close all she could see was the license plate. She screamed.

The driver yelled something and hit the gas. The car leaped forward but not far enough. The oncoming car hit the left fender of the cruiser.

The car went into a spin in the middle of the intersection. The driver whipped the steering wheel in the direction of the turn, struggling to keep them from overturning. That was the last thing she saw.

The spinning was too much for her. She closed her eyes. Dylan's arm painfully pressed against her waist, pushing her into the seat.

At long last the spinning began to slow. They came to a stop in the middle of the intersection. No one made a sound for a full minute. Joss opened her eyes.

The driver looked around in stunned amazement. "Everyone all right?"

Dylan leaned toward her. "Joss?"

She nodded. "I will be when my head stops spinning."

"I can't believe another vehicle didn't hit us. We're smack dab in the middle of the busiest street in Tucson." The driver was stunned.

"That's thanks to you, Officer. You saved our lives." Dylan's gaze jumped around. "Do you see the other car?"

"I saw it bounce off us, onto the curb and drive off. A hit-and-run. The rain must have blurred the driver's vision and he couldn't stop in time."

Dylan gave a shake of his head. "I'm not so sure."

"You think it wasn't an accident?" His words frightened Joss.

Dylan started to answer. He was turned her way as he spoke, and suddenly he grabbed for his gun holster and flipped up the cover. The gun was out and pointed toward someone running up to the car.

The driver lifted his hand. "It's okay. It's the officer from the car behind us."

Joss turned. She could see his vehicle parked not far from theirs, with its blue lights flashing. He ran to the window.

"Everybody okay?"

The driver rolled down their window. "Yeah. Just shaken up. I can't believe no one hit us."

Rain dripped off the lip of the man's cap. "I was able to get into the intersection and turn on my lights. I think that caught everyone's attention and gave them time to stop. But it was close."

"Did you get a good look at the car?" Dylan's tone was tense.

The officer looked at them. "Yes. I did. Older white Camry. The driver was a male with a baseball cap pulled low. I didn't get a good look at his face or the license plate. It happened too fast. I almost gave chase but this is a transport and it's more important to get our person delivered safely. I did report it before I came to check on you."

Even as he spoke, a siren echoed in the distance.

The driver turned to Dylan. "What do you want us to do? Return to the hospital or get to our destination?"

Dylan glanced at Joss. "Let's get her home safely. Hopefully another patrol car can catch our hit-and-run driver."

The officer jogged to his car, splashing through puddles in the middle of the intersection. Their driver rolled up his window and put the car in gear. Thankfully the vehicle moved into motion without a hitch.

Dylan squeezed her arm. Joss closed her eyes, willing the vertigo to ease. But it didn't. They were less than five minutes away from her apartment complex. They pulled into the parking lot. Beyond grass-covered hills, three-story buildings rose into the sky. As soon as the car came to a stop, Dylan helped her out. The vertigo had her spinning so much, he practically carried her across the grass, with the rain pounding on them.

By the time they climbed the two stories of stairs, her breath came in short, difficult gasps. A deputy pointed to the left. She turned a corner, concentrating on putting one foot in front of the other and leaned into Dylan. A dark brown door loomed in front of her. Holmquist opened it.

He frowned. "I heard about the hit-and-run. How are you?"

Joss didn't answer. Dylan squeezed her arm. "She's shaken up. Any sign of the car that hit us?"

Holmquist shook his head. "Not one, and we've got police cruisers on every street."

"I don't like the sound of that." Dylan gripped her arm tighter.

"Me neither. If it was a normal hit-and-run and the police units were that close, someone would have seen something. Since it just disappeared…"

"Sounds like another setup."

The men continued to talk, but Joss lost the thread of their conversation. Her eyes adjusted to the dark interior. A smell wafted over her. What was it? Dusty. Stuffy from being closed? Not a smell she recognized.

The apartment opened to a small kitchenette on the right. Four stools under a bar/counter. Black marble countertop. To the left a large bathroom. She peeked inside and glimpsed a connecting closet that opened into a bedroom. In front of her, a patio. Brightly colored pots with leafless branches sticking straight up. Obviously she killed living things.

Beside the couch, labeled boxes sat stacked on top of each other. One was labeled High School, the other Documents. She chewed her lip, then finally turned to Holmquist. "How long have I lived here?"

The men stopped talking and turned to her.

"About six months."

"But I still have boxes?"

Holmquist paused. "You work a lot. Devote yourself to the job."

"Obviously." Why was she disappointed? Because nothing jogged her memories? Because this place held no traces of home…of a life well lived? Or because that ticking clock, warning her of danger, continued its constant clanging in her head?

Her discomfort must have shown, because Holmquist said, "You're a good agent."

Now her smile was rueful. "So they tell me."

Dylan gave her arm a reassuring squeeze. Not even that helped.

Holmquist cleared his throat. "Jenny sent over some soup and stocked the fridge."

Jenny. Who was she? Obviously Joss's features looked as blank as her mind, because he added, "Jenny. Your friend."

Still blank.

Holmquist looked away. "She's the blonde agent. She came to see you in the hospital that first day. You two went to the academy together. You were roommates until she got married about six months ago and you moved here."

No image came to her. She didn't remember much of the first days. Only Dylan's voice.

Men were still trying to kill her...but now they were putting their own lives in danger to accomplish their goal. She couldn't imagine someone risking his own safety to ram the vehicle she traveled in. It was crazy or desperate. She didn't know which, because what she feared had happened. She'd returned to her apartment, and nothing, not a single thing, looked familiar.

She couldn't remember her past and the clock was still ticking. Something terrible was coming.

She closed her eyes and almost fell. "I need to lie down."

Dylan hurried to her side and wrapped his arm around her waist. Even that didn't help. "You need to sleep. That's what the doctor recommended."

Fear jumped in her stomach. "You'll be here when I wake up, right?"

"I'll be right here."

The vertigo was overwhelming and now her head began to pound viciously. Life...her life would have to wait one more day. She walked into the bedroom, rubbing her temples. Dylan pulled down a silky, dark brown comforter covered with beige paisley swirls. Was that her choice or standard for the apartment? She didn't like it much. Like everything else, it didn't fit.

She winced at the pain in her head, eased onto the pillows Dylan had puffed for her and closed her eyes. Just as he moved away, she grasped his hand and squeezed.

"Thank you. Don't know what I'd do if you weren't here."

If he answered, she didn't hear. The pounding took over.

FOUR

Joss opened her eyes. Morning, and for the first time since the cave-in, her head didn't hurt when she woke. Rising slowly, and anticipating a headache, she walked to the large bathroom. When no pain came, she flipped on the light.

An electric toothbrush stood beside the sink. She opened a drawer and looked through. She liked minty toothpaste, and not a lot of makeup. Tinted moisturizer. Mascara and a lipstick tube. Obviously she didn't spend much time with cosmetics. Cucumber-scented lotion sat on the counter. She found a bottle of perfume and spritzed it into the air.

Nice…but not familiar. Disappointment wiggled its way into the edges of her consciousness, but she refused to give in. Dr. Hull said to focus on what she knew, not what she didn't. Okay. She favored the scent of flowers and minty toothpaste…and she needed a shower. That was the agenda for this morning.

She left the bathroom with her hair dripping. The smell of bacon and eggs wafted into her room, and her stomach growled. Dylan's voice, lifted in a song, drifted in, along with the tantalizing aroma. She opened the bedroom door and winced at the bright sunlight shining through the sliding glass doors. She closed her eyes and paused, waiting for pain to slam her head. Nothing happened.

Maybe this would be a good day.

Dylan stood by the stove, with a pan in his hand. "Good morning. I've scrambled some eggs. Do you like them?"

"You tell me."

From across the room, his sigh was unmistakable. "I see frowns. Are you having a bad day?"

"Every day will be bad until I remember…if I remember."

Finally able to stop shielding her eyes, she saw the deep furrow crease his forehead.

He turned to the stove. "I prefer to think positive. For right now, sit and have something to eat."

She eased onto a high stool at the breakfast counter, waiting every moment for the headache to start again. When it didn't, a little of the worry slipped off her shoulders.

"Any word on the car that hit us?"

"No. Nothing yet. None of the cruisers spotted it on the streets. It disappeared…which makes me think it's a setup. Somewhere close by, someone is hiding that car." He shook his head. "It's too bad no one got the license plate."

Joss closed her eyes. The image of the license flashed in front of her. It looked like dirt had been smeared on it, but the rains had washed it away and she could see the number. "I did."

"What?"

"I looked up and it was right beside me." She shrugged. "Or maybe I'm good with numbers. Who knows?"

She rolled off the plate number and Dylan scrambled to punch it into his phone. He repeated it for confirmation.

"That's it."

"No. That's great! Thanks, Joss. I'll get this to Holmquist and maybe we'll have our first breakthrough."

His smile warmed her. For the first time she felt like a real agent…at least for a little while. Maybe today really *would* be a good day.

Dylan set scrambled eggs with salsa on the side in front of her. She scooped a little of the spicy sauce onto her eggs and took her first bite. The rich flavor of tomatoes and chilies rolled across her tongue.

"Ummm. This is good. I'll have to thank Jenny."

Dylan forked a bite into his mouth and shook his head. "This is all you. I found the open jar in your fridge."

She gave him a little nod and a slight smile. "Well, at least I know one thing I like."

"Joss, don't beat yourself up."

"I know. I know. Think about what I do know, not what I don't."

He lifted his glass of orange juice. "Good advice. Thank you, Dr. Hull."

She bit into a crunchy piece of bacon. "Thank *you* for breakfast."

"You're most welcome."

They ate in silence. When his plate was empty, Dylan pushed it aside and leaned forward. "Joss, you said last night you don't like storms. Do you remember why?"

She shook her head. "Nothing specific. Just a feeling. Bad things happen in storms."

He hung his head, obviously disappointed. When he looked up, his smile seemed forced. "I have to meet one of my agents this morning."

A sharp shaft of fear shot through her. How would she reach him? She shifted in her seat.

"I... I don't have a cell phone."

"No. Your phone and your service revolver were missing. We found no trace of either one when we cleared the tunnel. But don't worry, I won't leave until the protection detail arrives. There'll be two guards, one on the stairs outside and another at your front door. I'll ask them to check in on you frequently, but they'll be outside most of the time. They're not there now. Not while I'm here. By the way, that's a pretty comfy couch."

"I doubt if I picked it out. I don't seem to have much time for a homelife."

"You're a good—"

She lifted a hand. "Please don't say it. I've lost my revolver. That doesn't sound like the efficient officer you're trying to describe."

Dylan shook his head. "Don't expect too much too soon, Joss. Give yourself time."

"That's hard to do when I know people are trying to kill me." She paused as her sense of impending doom reared its head again. "I can't stop feeling like someone needs me or something is about to happen." She raised a hand. "And before you ask me, I don't know who or what. I just know something is going to happen and I need to stop it."

She met his level gaze. "Not to mention the fact that others are taking care of me. You're giving up your whole life. Don't you have a home, a place to be?"

"You are my 'place to be' right now, Joss." How she wished that were true. Wished she could relax and enjoy the home-cooked meals, the green-eyed gazes, the smiles and the hymns…especially the hymns. She wondered if he knew he sang. Nothing would make her feel better today than sitting on the couch and watching football with Dylan. Maybe it would bring back other memories…doing the one thing she knew they could do together.

And then cold washed over her in a shocking wave. Maybe Dylan had a woman in his life. Not a wife, because he wasn't wearing a ring, but a girlfriend…perhaps a fiancée. Someone he was neglecting so he could take care of her. Someone he had to explain to and make understand why he was spending every minute with a strange woman. Did he sing for her? Did she love his voice as much as Joss did?

All the times she had clung to him flashed through her mind. All his discomfort and sideways glances came back to her. The almost-guilty glances. Were they guilty because she counted on him so much and he had someone who needed and counted on him even more?

A rush of guilt overwhelmed her. She was doing it

again. Daydreaming about a relationship when so many other things were at stake.

Why can't I remember?

Someone knocked at her door, causing her to jump. Dylan saw her reaction. "It's just the officers coming to watch over you."

Clamping down on the fear tripping along her nerves, she nodded. Dylan answered the door. A man in a green border-patrol uniform stood outside.

"Henderson, what are you doing here? I thought one of the municipal police would be here."

The blond man gestured toward the patio. "He's on guard outside. I volunteered to take the second watch over Joss today."

Second watch. So many people being so kind. Did she deserve it?

Henderson looked over Dylan's shoulder. "Oh, hey, Joss. It's good to see you up."

The tone of his voice indicated he was another of the friends she couldn't remember. She wanted to slink away and pretend she didn't hear him. Instead she rose to her feet and walked to the door.

After what seemed to her like a very awkward pause, she put out her hand. "Hello. I take it we're friends."

Henderson's eyebrows rose in surprise. After a moment he smiled and gripped her hand in a firm shake. "Daniel Henderson. And yes, we are friends. We came up through the ranks together. Had a lot of postings at the same checkpoints. Together we've seen more of Southern Arizona than my wife and I have."

He grinned at his joke and tilted his head slightly,

almost as if he hoped the reminder would get a reaction. But Henderson, Jenny and all the others had disappeared into the gray mist of forgetfulness.

Henderson's smile faded. "Don't worry. You'll remember soon. We had some epic times together. No way will you forget those for good."

Joss smiled. She couldn't help herself. Henderson was likable and seemed like a good friend.

"I've got to get going." Dylan grabbed his wallet and keys off the counter. "I'll return later today. I can't give you a time, Joss."

She folded her arms across her chest, trying to hold herself together as he walked to the door. He hesitated. "You'll be all right."

She smiled quickly. Too quickly.

Dylan didn't seem to believe her either.

"What are you going to do?"

She lifted her lips in a smile, even if it was a bit shaky. "I'm going to spend the time meeting me."

Dylan smiled. All her discomfort washed away in his hazel-eyed glance…a look she already enjoyed too much. She stepped forward and pushed him out the door. "Go on. Get to work. I'll be fine."

After closing the door, she leaned against it.
If only I believed that.

Dylan said goodbye to Holmquist and turned on the ignition of his vehicle. Pausing to take the call from the supervisor was making him late for his appointment. But it was worth it.

Finally a real break in the case…and all because of Joss.

Holmquist had a name to go with the license plate she had identified. The car belonged to a woman named Lena Jones. Maybe they'd finally move forward on this case. He hoped so. They desperately needed a break, because it didn't appear that Joss's memory was going to return anytime soon.

Leaving her this morning was the last thing Dylan wanted to do. He hoped being home would trigger something. And he needed to be there when it did. That's why he regretted leaving this morning, not because she'd looked at him in fear, with her arms wrapped around herself in an attempt to hold it in.

And certainly not because of the slight cucumber scent that flowed around her. She smelled fresh, clean, reminding him of all the things he loved about summer. Swimming pools. His mother's garden. He hadn't thought of that in years. And he certainly didn't need to think of it now. Joss might be on the verge of remembering, and he needed to be there when she did. That was all.

But an image jumped into his mind… Joss clutching her arms around herself, trying to stop the trembling. Wincing when the thunder broke outside her window. Looking into his eyes with such trust—trust he wasn't sure he deserved. Dylan shook his head. Now wasn't the time to worry. Now was the time to focus. To find answers.

One of his agents, Manuel Gonzalez, had requested a meeting. Gonzalez had a female contact with important info, but she wanted a deal...something Gonzalez wasn't able to provide. Dylan had to meet with his agent and hear the info to determine if it was worth committing agency funds.

He turned into a downtown alley and pulled up to a brick building where neon letters flashed the words *The Silver Saddle Saloon*. Even in the bright Tucson sunlight, the neon sign was a beacon, drawing attention to the battered old building, which was surrounded by more of the same. Dylan pulled around to a small parking lot. His government SUV stood out like a sore thumb next to the beat-up economy cars filling the slots.

He looked around, searching each of the cars for occupants. All of the vehicles appeared empty. Still, his senses jangled. Was he walking into a trap? Gritting his teeth, he checked his Glock 17, then slipped it into the holster.

As he stepped out of his car, a cloud passed, blocking the heat of a hot August morning. The cloud presaged a monsoon shower later. The overcast sky added to the humid heat of a day already heading into triple digits. It also added to Dylan's tension.

Pausing at the rear door of the bar, he looked around. When he was sure no one loitered in the surrounding area, he headed inside. He paused, waiting for his eyes to adjust to the dark. The room was wide-open, almost empty. The bartender, leaning one elbow on the bar, turned to greet him. A patron with a shaved head, wearing a ball cap, lost interest in the TV above his head and turned to his drink. The bartender called out, "What can I do for you?"

Dylan ordered a soda and looked around. Gonzalez was seated at a small table that was tucked into a corner of the room…and he was alone.

Dylan looked around as he sat across from the other man. "Where's your contact?"

"She got nervous. She won't meet you until she's got your word that you'll help her get out of town."

"I can get her a bus ticket."

"She wants protection for her family…a son and her mom."

"That's a lot. Is her info worth it?"

"She says she knows Vibora's family and has information about his sister."

Dylan could not quell the hope that fired to life inside him. "Is she dependable?"

"I think so. She tells me she is…*was* the girl of one of Vibora's leaders, his second in command, Lucan Caulder. He threw her over for another woman, and left her high and dry with a kid. She wants out of the gang and she wants to do some damage on her way out. Says she knows Vibora's sister, who feels the same way. They talked at a party. The sister wants to get her mom and little sister as far from Vibora and his gang as possible. Says her brother's crazy."

"We can vouch for that. Nobody takes the risks he does." Dylan paused as the bartender walked toward them with his soda. Then he lingered, wiping the table next to them. Dylan waited until he walked away to speak again. "Any chance of a reconciliation between the two? I'm not going to invest in her only to have her run back to her ex."

The man shrugged. "I don't know. But my source says she's beat up pretty bad, with a black eye and a split lip. I do trust the man who sent her to me. He's given good information and been dependable in the past."

Dylan sipped his drink and took the opportunity to look at the bartender. He was bent close to the man with the baseball cap. From this angle, Dylan got a good look at the man's neck, where a tattooed serpent snaked its way up and disappeared beneath the cap.

An image flashed in Dylan's mind of the night outside Joss's hospital room. He never got a good look at the man who had tried to kill Joss. But he had tattoos in the same spots. Was this the same man?

Dylan rose to his feet. The bartender grasped the other man's arm. Dylan walked toward them. Behind him, he heard Gonzalez's chair scrape on the floor. The man with the tattoo tensed for action. Dylan did the same. When he was only a few feet away, the man spun around, knocking his bar stool to the ground and pulling a long knife from beneath his loose shirt in one movement. Before Dylan could react, the man lunged at him in the move he'd used in the hospital.

He is the same man!

All Dylan could do was dodge the knife, and he fell straight into Gonzalez. Moving quickly, his fellow agent kept them both from falling. Snake Man lunged again, sending Dylan and Gonzalez scrambling, almost tripping over their table. Neither man had time to unholster his gun.

The tattooed attacker dove for Dylan, who grabbed for the stool he'd stumbled over and swung. The rungs struck the man's outstretched hand, knocking the knife to the floor with a noisy clatter. The chair fell as well.

Out of the corner of his eye, Dylan saw the bartender moving, but he couldn't take his focus off the attacker in front of him. Gonzalez headed for the bar.

Snake Man lunged again. Dylan stepped back and then, after only a moment, moved toward the man, preparing to tackle him. But his attacker was ready. He shifted his position and swung his fist at Dylan's head with such force, it knocked Dylan to the ground. Dazed, he lay still and vulnerable.

"Hold it right there!" Dylan's attack on Snake Man had given Gonzalez enough time to pull out his gun. He moved it between the bartender and the man standing above Dylan.

But Snake Man wasn't done yet. He snatched the chair beside him and tossed it toward Gonzalez, who moved out of the way just in time. Gonzalez fired a shot, but it was high and wide. Snake Man spun for the door. After struggling to his feet, Dylan chased him.

Still feeling woozy, Dylan paused long enough to take out his weapon, then opened the door. Those precious minutes had cost him. The man had disappeared. Dylan ran into the parking lot, searched the street and all the nearby buildings, but saw nothing. The man had vanished.

Back inside, Gonzalez had his gun trained on the bartender. "I've already sent for backup."

Dylan gestured to the bartender to turn around so he could search him for a weapon. "Good. Now get on the phone and contact your witness."

Gonzalez nodded. "Lena Jones."

Dylan halted. "Your contact's name is Lena Jones?"

Now Gonzalez paused. "You know her?"

Excitement shot through Dylan. "I know her. Ask her if she owns a white Camry."

Gonzalez typed the message and waited for a response. "She says it's registered in her name, but Caulder took it. She hasn't seen it since they broke up."

Grim satisfaction filled Dylan. "Tell her to grab her son and her mother, pack a few things, and stay put. We're on our way."

Even if he had to go out on a limb, he would get the resources together to get the woman in protective custody. He would break the Serpientes, no matter the cost.

He took a breath. "But tell her I want that info now. I want the sister's name."

Gonzalez punched the message into his phone. A response came back in minutes. The agent studied the picture that flashed on his screen. Slowly he turned the phone so Dylan could see it.

Dylan recognized the woman from the files and photos his agents had gathered. Her name was Maria Martinez. She was the missing girlfriend of Jason Walker... Joss's brother.

Joss washed the breakfast dishes, plopped on the couch and then dozed. She jerked awake...agitated. She couldn't shake the sense that something needed to be done. Danger was just around the corner. That feeling hadn't eased since she'd left the hospital. If anything, it had grown stronger. She needed to do something. Now.

She looked around the apartment, and her gaze landed on the unpacked boxes by the couch. Surely those contained something of a more personal nature. She opened the first, labeled "high school" and found a yearbook from her senior year. She glanced through the pages and studied photos of her with friends. Not one person looked remotely familiar.

Henderson knocked on her door. He and his partner had been patrolling the grounds, but he'd checked on her frequently.

She unbolted the door and opened it. Her friend held a pizza box in his hands. "Chekowski…that's the guy out front…ordered pizza to be delivered. We thought you might want some."

The aroma drifted toward her, and her stomach grumbled. "I guess that's your answer." She glanced at the microwave's clock. "I had no idea it was lunchtime already."

"Well, this will do the trick. I know how much you like…" His words dropped off.

Another reminder of what she didn't know. Her discomfort must have shown on her face.

"Sorry, Joss. I didn't mean—"

Shaking her head, she took the pizza box from him. "It's all right. It's good to know I like—" she lifted the lid "—pepperoni pizza." She gestured him inside. "Come on in. I'll see if I can find something in the fridge to wash these down."

She found cans of soda stacked on one side of the refrigerator. Henderson chose two colas, then moved to the sliding glass door and held up one of them. "Chekowski?"

Joss joined him at the door. "I have a better idea. Let's move onto the patio."

Henderson stopped her at the door. "I'll stand out here, but you need to stay inside."

"I just…"

She stopped abruptly. Of course. Standing on her patio would make her an easy target for a shooter. Re-alization hit her slow and hard. She wanted to crawl into the bedroom and slink beneath the covers. Instead she slumped onto a nearby chair and handed the box to Henderson. Her appetite was gone.

He pushed it at her. "You need to eat, Joss. You've lost weight."

She glanced up. "Have I?"

Henderson grinned. "Yeah, and you were already too skinny. I've told you that a thousand times. A border-patrol officer needs to have some meat on them."

His teasing tone took the sting off the letdown of being a target. Henderson tossed the soda to Chekowski, who leaned over the outdoor stairwell, looking at them. He popped open the can. The two men chatted about the heat and the changing weather. Henderson talked about his new baby, who was only six weeks old. His wife had turned into a sleep-deprived zombie.

His descriptions made an image pop into her mind. Wistful images of a home flooded her…at least what she thought would make a good home. A sunny kitchen. Two big dogs sitting on the floor…maybe golden retrievers… and Dylan beside her. Green eyes that twinkled when he smiled. Wavy hair that always looked a little tousled. She'd still like to curl up on a couch with him. That thought continued to strike such a deep chord with her. Why?

Dylan was a friend, a larger-than-life knight in shining armor who'd swept in and wrapped his arms around her in the middle of a tornado. That was a far cry from husband material. At least, not the kind Joss kept seeing in her wishful dreams, the kind who cuddled on the couch, loved animals and got up each and every morning for a normal, sometimes even boring, job just because he loved his wife. That could never be Dylan.

"You're awful quiet." Henderson leaned against the doorjamb.

A small smile flitted over her lips. "I was thinking how great your life sounds. Like I'd like to crawl into it."

Henderson stepped across the room and crouched in front of her to grip her knee. "Listen to me. Your life is pretty great too."

"Really? What if I'm guilty?"

"Not one person on this force—no one who has worked with you—believes you've betrayed us. We know you had a good reason for being in that tunnel. That's why we are all so willing to fight for you."

"I'm not sure Dylan believes it."

Henderson flinched. "Murphy has his own battles to fight. Don't let yourself get caught up in them."

Too late. She was already "caught up." How Dylan felt about her already mattered too much. But Henderson's words reminded her of one thing. She could never allow her budding feelings for Dylan to grow. She could not drag him more deeply into the nightmare her life had become or might be in the future.

What if what the doctor had said was true and she never regained her memory? What if everything she knew and loved before had changed? What if she was a different person? Dylan deserved better. He deserved a woman who knew exactly who she was and what she wanted.

"I have to get out there. Chekowski's been in the heat too long. He needs a break." Henderson rose to his feet.

"I have to get to work too," she murmured.

Her friend smiled at her. "What's your work? Still meeting you?"

She gave him a wry twist of her lips. "Yep."

"Don't work too hard. You look like you could use some rest."

There would be no rest for her. Not until she figured out what was behind the ticking clock driving her crazy.

Henderson closed the door. She locked it behind him and then flopped onto the couch. The school yearbook lay open where she had left it. She flipped the page, and right in the middle was a picture of her in a long pink formal dress, with a crown on her head. She had her arm linked through that of a tall, good-looking, dark-haired man. The caption read "Prom Queen Jocelyn Walker Accompanied by Her Brother, Jason Walker."

She had a brother!

She flipped quickly through the rest of the pages, searching for another picture, but found nothing. Many people had signed the book but they were all generic statements like "best wishes." Nothing personal that said anything about the real Joss Walker. Apparently she hadn't had many attachments in school. That explained why her brother had accompanied her to the prom and not another young man.

Sounded like her high school life was about the same as her current life. Lots of work. Well-liked with many acquaintances—enough to elect her prom queen—but not many close friends.

She dug through the rest of the box and found a dried corsage, a class pin and a ring. Some school papers, awards for good grades. Things that meant nothing to her…brought no memories or flashes of recognition. She slid the top box to the floor and pulled open the one beneath. Inside she found a metal box full of important documents.

Her birth certificate. She was twenty-seven years old. Good to know. She shook her head at the craziness of not knowing her own birth date. Then she stumbled across a death certificate. Clipped to it was a newspaper article about how John Walker, owner and operator of Walker's Corner Store, had been shot and killed in an attempted robbery at his place of business.

Her father had been murdered. She waited for the emotions that should have come with that knowledge. Sorrow. Anger. Loss. But the only emotion the knowledge generated was guilt for not feeling more. The words on the paper meant nothing. Except that they might explain her devotion to law enforcement.

Filed behind it was another death certificate, this one for Anna Walker, and a newspaper obituary. She had died of a rare kidney ailment when Joss was sixteen. The article said Anna was survived by her son and daughter.

Nothing. No memories. No emotions.

Pictures. She needed pictures. Something! Someone!

Where are you, Jason Walker? Why did you leave me all alone? Are you in danger? Do you need my help?

The pounding in her head returned so strongly, she could hardly bear it. As she closed the small metal container, a document with gold scrollwork caught her eye. Her baptismal certificate. She'd been baptized not long after her mother had died. Obviously she'd found comfort in her faith during that period of mourning. Why hadn't she found comfort now? Why couldn't she remember anything of her faith, except for the words of a few old hymns?

The pounding drowned out the rest of her thoughts, and she sagged to the floor with the certificate clutched in her hand. She buried her face in her arms as hot tears squeezed beneath her lids.

Where are You, God? Why have You abandoned me...like everyone else in my family?

Dylan hated being away from Joss a minute longer but he needed to eat. The way this day was going, if he didn't do it now, it might not happen.

He headed to a drive-through and ordered. Armed with a bag full of cheeseburgers and fries, he nodded to the uniformed officer at the base of the stairs to Joss's apartment, then took the steps two at a time. Henderson stood outside her door.

"How is she?"

"Not a peep out of her. I think she's resting. We ordered some pizza and she's been quiet ever since."

Dylan smiled and held up the bag. "Good to know. I picked up a couple of extra burgers, but now I can eat them myself." He knocked on the door. The bolt slammed back and the door jerked open. Joss stood before him, with tear streaks on her cheeks, and her ponytail awry.

"I have a brother. Why hasn't he been to see me?"

Dylan's smile faded. He glanced toward Henderson, who shrugged with a droll look. Dylan stepped inside and closed the door. He held up the bag. "I brought food. Can we eat first?"

"I'm not hungry."

"I am and I've had a long day. Give me a second and I'll try to explain."

"What is there to explain? What's wrong with my brother?"

Dylan moved past her and set the bag on the breakfast bar. After unrolling the top, he began to set out the food.

"Was he injured too? Is he dead? Is that why you are stalling? It has to be bad. Otherwise you wouldn't be trying to keep it a secret."

He eased onto the stool and shook his head. "It's not a secret, Joss. It's just…we don't know where Jason is. He's missing."

"What do you mean?"

"I mean he's missing. He hasn't shown up for work. He's not in his apartment or answering his cell. Even his girlfriend and her family have disappeared. We've been trying to track them down, but so far…" He shrugged.

Joss eased onto the stool beside him. "You aren't keeping the truth from me, are you? Was he in that tunnel with me? I can handle it if he was." She looked at her hands, and Dylan's gaze followed hers. Her fingers were clenched so tightly, the knuckles were white. "At least one question will be answered."

Her quietly spoken words pierced Dylan like a knife. Her fear and confusion was tearing at him.

"He wasn't in the cave-in and we don't have answers, Joss. We don't know what's going on."

"The girlfriend's whole family is missing?"

"Yes. Maria, her mother and her little sister."

She shook her head. "I don't understand. How could they be missing and no one knows anything about them?"

"We don't have those answers, but we have had our first breakthrough with an informer named Lena Jones. And thanks to your good memory of the license plate, we traced the car that hit us to her."

"The driver of the car yesterday was a woman?"

Dylan shook his head, his mouth full of food. "No. It was a man. She says her ex-boyfriend had been making payments on it, so when they split, he took it and she hasn't seen it since."

He paused. "The boyfriend's name is Caulder. Ring any bells?"

She frowned. "No. Not a one."

Dylan was hesitant to feed her all of the information at one time. He didn't want to lead her. He wanted her to remember on her own. He felt a twinge of guilt for his omissions. But too much too soon might bring back the headaches, and she seemed on the verge of a breakthrough…at least that's what he hoped.

She placed a hand on his arm. "I have this feeling that something horrible is about to happen. I can't shake it and now you tell me Jason is missing. What if he's been in an accident and I was going to him? What if…"

Dylan shook his head, anxious to ease her fears. "It looks like your brother packed for some kind of trip. Toiletries are missing—things like that."

Joss was silent. He could almost see the wheels turning behind her beautiful gray-toned gaze.

"If he's taking a trip, we can trace it through his bank account, right? Plane or train tickets. Gas or money withdrawals throughout the country."

Dylan dropped his hamburger, a little surprised that she was putting two and two together so quickly. She was starting to sound like the old Joss. He was glad. He'd missed her quick mind and sharp observations.

"We've put in the request to access his accounts, but the warrant hasn't been approved yet."

She sagged and then grasped his arm again. "All the more reason why I have to go to my brother's apartment. I have to remember. All I need is to walk through. Surely he has pictures. Mementos. More than this." She gestured to her utilitarian apartment.

Dylan picked up his hamburger and shook his head. "I told you. We searched the place. If there was something there, we would have found it."

She bit her lip. "I don't mean a clue. I mean something that will trigger my memory." She gestured around the room. "Look at this place. There's nothing here. I don't really live here. My brother has a real life. He's got a girlfriend."

Dylan chuckled. "If that qualifies a person for a real life, then I've failed too."

She didn't laugh or smile. Her pointed stare hit him right between the eyes and told him exactly what she thought. He ducked his head, not willing to engage in a discussion about his own seemingly joyless, utilitarian life.

She turned away and Dylan was able to take another bite. But it looked like it would be his last, because Joss shook her head.

"That thought gives me no comfort. Something is terribly wrong. Something is about to happen and my memory is the key. I have to do something. I need to go."

She turned to him. "Please, Dylan. Take me to my brother's apartment."

He shook his head and swallowed rapidly.

"I can't, Joss. I have to get to my office and process paperwork. We have to get Lena Jones, her son and her mother to another location. Day after tomorrow we're transferring her to another city, hopefully one that's out of state."

"Please, Dylan. All I need is a quick walk-through. After that, Henderson and Chekowski can bring me home. You can go straight to your office. For that matter, things have been quiet here. Henderson and Chekowski can take me."

Those words jolted an immediate reaction. "No way. If you go, I'm going with you."

Hope flared in her eyes. "Does that mean you'll take me?"

Dylan hesitated. If a visit to the apartment triggered Joss's memory, it would be fantastic. Any information she gave them, coupled with Lena Jones's revelations, could break this case wide-open. And Joss was right, Jason Walker and Maria Martinez could be in danger.

He resolutely refused to admit that his main reason for considering the visit would be to ease Joss. She needed some relief, some help, and if it was in his power, he wanted to give it to her. He was a bit concerned about how badly he wanted that. But that was another matter for another time.

Fifteen minutes across town. Fifteen in Walker's apartment and the same for the return. Gonzalez had already picked up Jones and was taking her to a secure hotel. Dylan could spare the time. If he couldn't get the necessary paperwork done in time for the transfer, he'd put Jones's tickets and hotel on his own credit card.

He set his food down, opened the door, stepped outside and closed it behind him. He called the two guards together and told them what Joss had proposed.

Henderson shook his head. "No way. It's too dangerous."

The uniformed policeman Joss called Chekowski was silent for a long while. Then his features hardened. "Let's go. She might find something they missed."

Henderson shook his head. "You're crazy too."

Chekowski shrugged. "We have the advantage of

surprise. Do you really think that gang is watching this place 24/7? We'll be in and out before those creeps know she's left the apartment."

The men turned to Dylan, waiting for his decision.

It was a risk. He was going out on a limb. But it would be worth it if even one object in the apartment helped Joss regain her memory. Watching her struggle in a world she didn't recognize bothered him more than he cared to admit to his fellow officers…maybe even to himself.

"Let's do it."

FIVE

Joss stopped at the foot of the stairs outside her apartment. The heavy heat of the Tucson summer hit her full force. It was like a blast from a furnace, and she sucked in her breath. Weakness slipped over her and she had to pause.

Chekowski's heavy tread echoed behind her, and his bulky shadow fell on the ground in front of her. "Are we doing this or not?" His impatience spurred her into action.

"Which way?"

He pointed to a police car parked in the closest parking slot. "You're riding in my car. Murphy says it's the most fortified."

Dylan and Henderson stood in the parking lot, conversing. They had searched the parking lot and the whole area before they allowed her to leave her apartment. As they crossed the grass, Chekowski pulled out his cell and typed out a message with his thumbs. "We won't need backup, but I'm letting my supervisor know what's going on." He punched the send button and then slid his cell phone into his pocket.

Chekowski opened the passenger door of the front for her, but Dylan jogged toward her and motioned to the back. "Joss, get in the back with Henderson. I'll sit in the front."

Nodding, she opened the door and slid in. The car was like an oven and it smelled. Not like a car with leather and upholstery...but like sweat and fear.

Chekowski started the engine and cranked on the air conditioner, but very little reached her. Nausea threatened to overwhelm her.

Not now! Not after I fought so hard to get here.

Dylan gave Chekowski the address and he plugged it into the GPS on the console. The screen on the console read Fifteen Minutes Until Arrival. She closed her eyes and tried to calm herself.

She had begun to relax when they bumped into a parking lot. A scraggly saguaro with ragged, bug-eaten arms posed in front of a sign that said Saguaro Sunset Apartments. Both looked in danger of toppling over. In one corner of the lot, a car with four missing tires rested on blocks of wood.

Dylan opened the door and she stepped out. One side of the older three-story brick apartment building was covered in graffiti. A gang symbol caught Dylan's attention and he walked toward it. A striped snake with a lashing tongue curved around a large block letter *S*.

"You know this symbol?"

Dylan did. "It means this is Serpientes territory."

"And my brother lives right in the middle of their claim?"

Dylan nodded.

A monsoon cloud passed over, bringing with it the dark hint of a storm. The breeze came up suddenly in the afternoon heat. Joss shivered. "How long has he lived here?"

"Almost twelve years. You moved here together after your mother passed. He never moved away."

Twelve years. Her brother had been negotiating these dangerous waters for all of those years? Could he really have stayed free from entanglement in all of that time? Or had he succumbed? Fallen victim to the gang's promises of protection, wealth or safety? She didn't know. Didn't remember anything about her brother. She could only hope she'd find answers in his apartment.

They entered the small lobby. Mailboxes lined one wall. In front of them was an elevator with a handwritten sign taped to the metal door. The sign read Out of Order.

Dylan snapped the cover on his holster loose. "I don't like this."

Chekowski pulled his weapon too. "We've come this far. Might as well go the rest of the way."

Henderson nodded and Dylan pointed to one end of the narrow lobby. "Stairwells bracket both ends of the building. Walker's apartment is closer to the right, so we'll go that way."

They started up. The stairwell smelled like cooked cabbage. What was it with her sense of smell today? It seemed to overwhelm every other sense and added to her discomfort.

Their footsteps echoed in the empty stairwell. They walked quietly, but the sound pounded into Joss's head. By the time they reached the third floor, she was breathing heavily and the pounding had turned into a full-fledged headache.

Chekowski took the lead. He opened the door and peered down the empty hallway. "Let's go."

Dylan followed, with Joss close behind him. Henderson trailed. Chekowski's body blocked Joss's view of the hall ahead, but the apartment doors they passed showed the age and well-worn look of the rest of the complex.

Why did Jason live in this run-down place? Couldn't he afford anything better? She could understand if he was a young man who was struggling to raise a younger sister, but where did his money go now that she had her own job and means of support?"

So far this trip had brought more concerns than answers.

Suddenly a door just ahead and to the right opened a crack. Joss glimpsed a young teen boy before an older man's face appeared. The door slammed shut and the dead bolt slid into place. Dylan came to an abrupt halt. Then he spun, grabbed Joss's shoulder and pushed her back the way they'd come.

"The neighbors are worried. Something's not right. Turn around." His harsh whisper broke the silence of the empty hall. Startled, Joss obeyed. Henderson ran ahead of her. Only when they reached the door of the stairwell did she pause long enough to look back.

The door to her brother's apartment suddenly burst open. A man with a long black beard appeared in the doorway. He ran toward them as Dylan shoved her into the stairwell and slammed the door behind them. A two-by-four, long enough to prop the door open, leaned against the wall. Dylan grabbed it and jammed it against the knob.

"Go! Get to the car."

Something hit the door with a thud, but the board held. Henderson grabbed her arm and pulled her down the stairs. They rounded the corner of the second-floor landing. Two little girls, one with a ball in her hand, stepped into the stairwell.

"Get back! Go home and hide!" Henderson shouted as he dragged Joss down the next flight. The girls screamed and ran, dropping the ball so it bounced down the stairs. Joss almost tripped over it, but Dylan came from somewhere behind her, scooped her up by the waist and dragged her until she got her footing again.

Above them a loud crash echoed through the stairwell…the wooden board clattered on the steps. The man with the beard—along with his accomplices, if he had any—was in the stairwell.

Dylan pushed her against the wall so she was out of range of anyone from above. They never slowed their steps. A shot exploded and reverberated through the stairwell. Joss glanced up. The man with the beard leaned over the upper railing, taking aim again. Dylan stopped, aimed and fired. The man ducked out of sight.

Dylan stayed behind. Henderson tugged her down one more flight and out the stairwell door to the lobby.

Joss halted, waiting for Dylan. He burst through the door, grabbed Joss's hand and dragged her to the exit. Then, with a quick movement, he gestured for her to wait inside. Stepping out into the parking lot, he looked around, then turned to face the apartment windows above. He gave her the "all clear" gesture and motioned her to the police car. "Get to the other side. Hide behind a tire and don't raise your head unless I tell you."

Joss obeyed. All three men followed her. Using the car as a shield, they ducked and faced the entrance of the building.

Minutes passed and nothing happened. Dylan's voice was low and raspy. "Chekowski, did you radio for backup yet?"

Only then did the policeman reach for the radio attached to his shoulder. A thought trickled through Joss's mind, but she lost it as a gray Toyota truck screeched from behind the apartment complex and shot out into the street. Dylan pounded the car with his fist and ran down the street, chasing the truck.

After a few yards, he returned. "Sooner or later I'm gonna catch that guy."

The cooler temperatures of night slid over Dylan, a relief from the sweat-drenching temperatures of the day. Still, as he turned on the engine, he hit the air conditioner. Cold air blew over him and he closed his eyes, allowing himself a moment before he shifted the car into gear and drove out of the station.

His team had accomplished a lot since this morning's meeting with Gonzalez. Using info from Lena

Jones, they'd tracked down records and photos of the gang members she had identified. Now information was starting to roll in almost faster than they could process it. The investigation was moving forward.

Unfortunately things were at a standstill for Joss. The trip to Jason Walker's apartment hadn't broken through the wall that hid her past. After reinforcements had arrived, he'd taken her through the place. Nothing triggered her memories. Frustrated, she'd grasped a photograph of her brother and Maria Martinez off the counter and clutched it to her chest, almost as if she needed it to remember her brother's face.

The information Dylan had received was going to upset Joss even more. Jason Walker had been an engineering major. One of his professors remembered him as a bright student and was severely disappointed when Walker dropped out.

Files on Jason Walker's bank account had also arrived. Over the past year, he'd been paid sixty thousand dollars in three separate payments, several months apart. The day before Joss's accident, he withdrew all the money and closed the account.

Dylan suspected that Jason Walker agreed to use his engineering knowledge to build the tunnels for the Serpientes. Then he used Vibora's own money to help Maria and the rest of her family escape her brother's violent gang life.

Even if his suspicions were correct, it didn't answer the questions about Joss. Did she know about her brother working for the gang and try to cover for him? Is that how she ended up in the tunnel? Or did they try to kill her because she didn't know her brother's location and was of no use to them?

Whatever their reasons were, Dylan's opinion of Joss's brother was sinking by the minute. Walker had abandoned his sister to face Vibora and his wrathful actions alone.

An image of Joss's pale features, smiling, telling him she would be all right when she was so obviously terrified, flashed into his mind and sent a surge of anger surging through him.

She didn't deserve this. None of it. And if her desperate "ticking-clock need" came from a desire to help her brother, his betrayal would sink deep and maybe even destroy her.

Dylan's jaw clenched. More than ever he wanted to get Vibora, Caulder and anyone else involved with this gang. His grip on the wheel tightened and he almost ran a red light.

Slamming on the brakes, he shook his shoulders loose. He was losing his laser-like focus because of his overriding need to protect Joss. He *would* get the Serpientes and everyone connected to them. It was his job. He couldn't forget that and he couldn't let his emotions cloud his investigation. No matter how hard he tried, these new, fierce feelings for Joss kept overriding his control. He might have been attracted to her before, but nothing compared to the emotions she triggered now. Her honesty and vulnerability grabbed him by the throat and wouldn't let go. If he wasn't careful, those feelings would lead him down the wrong path.

He had more important information to focus on than

Joss's disillusionment with her brother...like the hit-and-run attack on the police vehicle. There was still no trace of the white Camry. Then today the Serpientes member had appeared at his meeting with Gonzalez. How did the gang know about the meeting, let alone the exact details of where and when?

That was one too many coincidences. Dylan didn't believe in coincidences. Today's fiasco at Walker's place proved he was right not to. Those gang members were waiting to ambush them. His jangling senses and the click of a watchful neighbor's door were the only things that had saved them.

Somehow, someway, the gang was getting information about their movements. He was sure of it. But how? And who was leaking their plans?

He pulled into the parking lot at Joss's apartment. Gathering his cell phone and a pile of files from the passenger's seat, he hurried to greet Chekowski. The officer was still on duty at the base of the stairs, and Henderson met him at the top. A major accident downtown had left the police department short of officers, so they could not provide extra men to replace Henderson and Chekowski. Fortunately both men had agreed to stay.

"Thanks for holding down the fort until I could get here. I appreciate it."

Henderson nodded. "No problem. We'll stick around for another half hour or so. Give you a chance to relax before you're on watch."

Dylan shook the man's hand. "I appreciate that. It's been a wild day."

With his hands full, he knocked on the door. Joss opened it cautiously. She looked worn-out, fragile, like she had in the hospital. Fear jumped into his heart.

"How are you feeling?"

She sent him a wry look over her shoulder as she let him in. "As best as can be expected for someone with no memories."

"No headaches?"

"Nothing since we left Jason's apartment. That's a good thing, I guess."

Dylan released a small sigh of relief. That wry look did much to ease his concern. Some of the old Joss was starting to resurface, and he couldn't believe how happy he was to see her.

A pizza box sat on the corner of the counter. "The guys ordered out again. We saved you some. Are you hungry?"

"Starving."

"I'll warm it up."

She slid several pieces onto a paper plate and put it in the microwave. "So, did you get your informant settled in? Did she give you a lot of info?"

"And then some. More than we could process in one afternoon."

"That good?"

Should he tell her? Was she healthy enough to start hearing the facts? A part of Dylan wanted to say no, to tell her nothing had come of the interview. He was tired mentally and physically. Sitting at the counter, just talking, sounded great to him. The best ending to a difficult day.

Hadn't he had this argument with himself and decided to put these misguided feelings behind him? Stomping on them, he plopped his phone and the folders on the counter.

"You tell me." He pulled a photo out of a file. "This is Caulder. Does the picture jog any memories?"

Joss pulled it toward her and spun it around. She studied the photo for a long while, and all the while she rubbed a spot above her temple with two fingers of one hand.

She shook her head and pushed it to him. "No. Just some uncomfortable feelings."

He handed her another photo, this one of Vibora with his slicked-back man-bun and tattoos slithering over both arms. "How about this guy?"

Her breath caught and she frowned. "No clear memories, but there's…something about him… I don't know. He frightens me. Does that mean something?"

Dylan didn't answer…didn't want to lead her. She needed to find the memories for herself. He pulled out several more, including one of Lena Jones and Vicente Aguilar, aka Snake Man. But nothing looked familiar. She pulled Caulder's photo across the counter one more time, then shook her head.

"This guy doesn't just make me uncomfortable. He scares me too. I don't know why, but he does."

Dylan paused. "Think carefully, Joss. If you know anything about him…can connect him in any way to you or your presence at the tunnel, it would be all I'd need to pick him up for questioning."

She frowned and studied the picture.

Frustrated, he gave up hoping she would remember on her own and prompted her. "Caulder is Lena Jones's ex-lover. He took her car and used it to ram us yesterday. He's Vibora's second in command."

Joss looked up.

"That's right. Lena has known both Caulder and Mario Martinez, aka Vibora, since they were kids." He paused, waiting to see if she drew the connection between Mario and her brother's girlfriend, Maria. He saw nothing, not a flicker of recognition.

Disappointed, he went on. "They grew up in the same neighborhood. That's why she's so bent about Caulder's abandonment. She's been with him since the beginning. When she found out he was cheating on her, it was the final straw. She decided to turn on him."

He paused. "Lucan Caulder and Mario Martinez have rap sheets as long as my arm." He repeated Vibora's name one more time, just for emphasis, but still she didn't make the connection.

He sighed. "Mario Martinez's sister is Maria…your brother's girlfriend."

Her lips parted and her gaze widened. "My brother has ties to the Serpientes?"

"Yes."

"Oh, no." She walked to the couch and plopped down. Barely catching the edge of the cushion, she slid to the floor. With her knees bent, she closed her eyes and massaged both temples.

Had her headaches returned, or was it a nervous habit? Should he move cautiously or blaze forward? He'd had this argument with himself before. Time was running out. He couldn't afford to protect Joss anymore. He had to go on.

After stepping over her slender body, which was curled up on the floor, he sat on the sofa above her. "There's more. In college your brother studied engineering...specifically mining engineering...before dropping out to take care of you. He was close to finishing before he was forced to quit."

She stopped rubbing her head and looked at him. "Are you suggesting that my brother built the gang's tunnels?"

"We've compared the timeline to his relationship with Maria Martinez. They've been together for two years. About six months ago, Jason started to deposit substantial amounts of money into his bank account. Not long after that, the tunnels started to appear. Joss, the deposits equal more money than he could have earned at his mechanic job."

A deep frown appeared between her brows, the same one he'd seen when she had a headache. Had he gone too far, pushed too hard?

Before he could ask, he heard a noise outside. "What was that?"

"I didn't hear anything."

"It sounded like something fell on the ground."

He started to rise from his seat when a shout outside the door echoed through the hall. A shot exploded. Joss cried out and covered her ears. Dylan slid to his knees, beside her, and pulled his weapon from the holster.

Joss moved as if to rise, but Dylan pushed her down. "Stay here."

Adrenaline rushed through his fatigued body. He flipped open the lock of his gun. Another shot rang out. This time the bullet pierced the door and zinged across the room. Joss cried out again.

Dylan paused for a moment, then rushed to the door, threw it open and aimed, hoping to catch the shooter off guard. A man with a baseball cap was running toward him, halfway down the long hall. He fired at Dylan, who dodged behind the wall of Joss's apartment.

Henderson had fallen to the ground. Semiconscious, he slumped sideways into the doorway, blocking it. Dylan couldn't shut the door, nor drag him in. They were both sitting ducks. He had to make a move.

From behind the shelter of the wall, Dylan leaned out and fired another shot at the man, who was still running toward the door. The shot ricocheted off the wall near the man's head. He spun and fled the way he'd come.

Dylan stepped over Henderson and raced after him. The man with the baseball cap paused, turned and fired. Dylan crouched and lunged sideways, banging into one of the doors in the hall. Someone shouted from behind the door.

"Hey! What's going on out there?"

"Stay inside and call the police!"

The running man was almost to the end of the hall by the time Dylan recovered. As the man passed one of the hall lights on the wall, Dylan saw the distinctive snake tattoo on the back of his neck.

Anger surged through him. This time he was going to get Snake Man.

He powered on the speed. Snake Man turned the

corner and dashed down the stairs. Glass shattered. Dylan paused at the shadowy corner and peeked over. Snake Man had broken all of the lights. The stairwell was completely dark. His assailant could be waiting and taking aim now. Jerking behind the protection of the corner, he checked his weapon.

Dylan glanced around. Joss was leaning over Henderson in the open doorway. Chekowski was nowhere to be seen. Was he injured too? Snake Man could even now be circling around the building and heading up those unguarded stairs!

He pushed away from the wall and ran toward Joss. Just then, he heard the sound of an engine revving. The deep rumble of the motor reverberated through the empty hall, pounding against Dylan's ears. His heart pounded with it.

Joss pressed a kitchen towel to Henderson's shoulder, trying to stop the bleeding. She'd been dreading a terrible incident, and now one had happened. The gang was mowing down innocent people. Officers…good people were being hurt, and someway, somehow, she felt as if she could have prevented this.

Henderson groaned as she pressed his wound, but she barely heard it. There was a louder sound, one that drowned out all else. A powerful engine revved. She looked up. The vertical blinds on the sliding glass door were closed, but a bright light flashed through the slight crevices…as if someone had shined a spotlight on the doors. The engine revved louder…and closer…like it was below her window.

Rapid gunfire exploded through the air. Bullets pierced the sliding glass doors, shattering them and ripping across the entire apartment.

Joss screamed and flung herself over Henderson's body. Bullets tore across the room, destroying everything in their path. They zinged over her head...straight to the outside door and Dylan's running figure.

She screamed his name before another round of bullets shredded the apartment, chipping pieces of the doorjamb and sending splinters everywhere. Joss ducked again, shielding Henderson's head and face.

When the next round of rapid gunfire paused, she lifted enough to see that Dylan was safe...crouched waiting for the hail of bullets to ease.

The gunfire started again, but this time it was aimed at the bedroom. Bullets tore into the window and destroyed that room as well. The engine revved again. Lights flashed and the vehicle sped off.

Most of the vertical blinds had been ripped in two or torn away, but a few remained, still swinging from the violent spray of bullets. Glass had been blown all the way across the room and littered the ground around her. She stared at it in stunned silence.

"Joss! Are you all right? Joss!"

Once again Dylan's voice anchored her, brought her to her senses. She rose to her feet and dashed into his arms. He pulled her to his chest. Nothing had ever felt so good. She tucked her face into his neck and sobbed her relief.

"I was afraid you'd been hurt," he murmured.

She shook her head. "I was on the floor. But you

could have been hit. Those bullets went right through the door."

He took a slow breath. "God was watching out for both of us."

His words penetrated the haze of fear in her mind. Was the Lord truly watching out for her? Was it possible He hadn't abandoned her?

Sirens stopped outside the apartment complex, and blue lights flashed along the walls. Dylan tried to push her away, but she would not release him. Not yet. She should let him go do his job, but her world was still reeling and she needed him. Besides, he didn't seem all that determined to release her. Pulling her along, he scooted to the edge of the stairwell and shouted down to the approaching officers. Standing up, he saw Chekowski's unconscious body lying at the foot of the stairs.

"We're up here. Henderson's been shot and your man is down. We need an ambulance."

Multiple officers ran toward them, their guns drawn. One stopped to examine Chekowski, who appeared unconscious but otherwise unharmed. Other officers ran up the stairs. One man paused where Dylan and Joss stood while two more carefully searched her shattered home.

She clung to Dylan as he related the events to the lead officer. The others signaled that the apartment was clear, and the emergency technicians ran up the stairs with a gurney. The whole time Joss held on to Dylan. Only when they loaded Henderson onto a stretcher and headed to the stairs was she able to release Dylan.

She ran to her friend and grasped his hand. He seemed alert. "I'm so sorry."

She clung to his hand as they carried him out. "I'll be all right, Joss," he promised, releasing her hand. "I'll be all right. Don't worry." His fingers slid from hers.

Don't worry? How could she not? She looked around at the blood on the cement floor of the landing, at the bullet holes in the wood and stucco outside her door. No matter how many times people said it wasn't her fault, she couldn't shake the feeling that it was. Guilt rode on her shoulder and she couldn't seem to shrug it loose.

Dylan and the officer in charge had moved into the kitchen. Like a sleepwalker, Joss shuffled into her living room.

Glass was spread across her couch. She gingerly brushed the thick pieces off a corner and sat on the edge. Wrapping her arms around herself, she leaned over her lap.

Lord, if You are listening... I need You. Need to stop people from being hurt, stop the destruction. I don't know who I was or what I did, but these people are being hurt because of me. Help me. Tell me who I am. Help me stop this!

Tears rolled down her cheeks and onto her knees. She let them fall until a breeze wafted into the room. Cool, crisp and comforting, like the breath of God. Words came to her mind.

Persecuted, but not forsaken; cast down, but not destroyed.

It was a scripture. She knew it. She couldn't remember her past, any of her life, but God's word echoed in her mind, telling her the truth. He had not abandoned her.

Her spirit came alive and peace filled her. She lifted her head, let the breeze brush over her heated cheeks like an unseen caress.

She was not alone. She was a beloved child of God.

She might not have a family, be a good sister or a good agent, but she was a child of God's Kingdom. Dylan was right. The Lord had been watching over her, right from the cave-in, until now. She knew it, felt it in the marrow of her bones.

She might never remember. Her future might never be linked to her past. She might even be guilty of… something. But she was on the right path. He was guiding her and would never leave her.

She'd been clinging to Dylan. All the while the One she needed to cling to had been silent…waiting for her to remember she was not alone.

"Joss?" Captain Holmquist walked into the room.

Rising, she wiped the tears from her cheeks. His rugged features were wreathed in worry. They seemed suddenly very dear to her…like the father she couldn't remember. Feelings of affection rushed over her, and she hurried into his open arms. He crushed her in a hug.

Glass crunched. Her supervisor released her and they turned. Dylan walked toward them.

"This is a disaster, Murphy. We've got to get her out of this mess. Someplace where they can't find her."

Dylan ducked his head. "I think I might know a spot."

"Where?"

"My place."

Holmquist shook his head. "How is your apartment going to be any safer than this one?"

"Not here. I mean my family's ranch. It's in the San Pedro River Valley southeast of Tucson. Two hours away. It's pretty isolated, and it's been empty for years."

"Empty? Is it habitable?"

"It better be. I pay a cleaning company to give it a once-over every year. They just finished a few days ago. The electricity and phone are still on. I haven't had time to call and shut them off."

The captain frowned. "But you haven't been there?"

He shook his head. "Not since my parents left." He looked down. "Too many bad memories. After I graduated and moved to Washington, they put the ranch in my name and moved to California. The place has been in our family for generations so I'm reluctant to sell it."

"But you're willing to go there now, for me?" Joss shook her head. She couldn't let him do it. The bad memories had to be related to his dead sister. It was too much and too many people had already been hurt. "I can't ask you to do that."

Dylan shrugged. "It's the perfect place. We'll put the word out that I've been called to Washington. No one will make the connection to my absence and my home in the valley."

Holmquist nodded. "You can't just drive out of here. They've probably got someone watching this place."

"We'll need a decoy."

"Agreed. I'll call Jenny."

Joss fisted her fingers. "No. I won't have her or anyone else hurt because of me."

Holmquist squeezed her arm. "It's all right, Joss. We'll dress her in a wig and different clothes. You'll leave in that wig and clothes. Later Jenny will come out of your apartment in her own hair and uniform, looking like any other border-patrol agent. They'll think you are still inside. Jenny will never be in danger."

Joss looked around at her shattered apartment...a good reflection of her life.

It was time for a change, time for her to start her new path.

"All right. I'm ready."

The window in her bedroom was shattered, the blinds ripped apart, just like in the living room. The light on the ceiling hadn't been hit. It shone like a spotlight on the mess, and out the open window, into the black night. Joss didn't like the idea that everyone outside could see her. The men who did this might be watching.

Glass littered the bed, but she lifted a corner of the spread and tumbled all the shards to one side. Then she hung the heavy brown spread over the curtain rod. Only then did she go to the closet, where she found a duffel-type suitcase, beginning to throw clothes inside it.

Just as she zipped the bag closed, Dylan stuck his head in the door and jutted his chin toward the window. "I see you had the same idea."

He pulled the top blanket off her bed and headed toward the living room. She followed and watched him loop the heavy blanket on the curtain rod to block the view.

"They're watching us right now, aren't they?"

"So far they've known every move we've made. Either they're watching...or..." He didn't finish his sentence, but he glanced at the police gathered around, talking to Holmquist. "We have to make sure we keep our plans to ourselves."

That was a new and terrifying thought. These people...all of them...had been incredibly kind to her. Henderson had taken a bullet while protecting her. Chekowski had been knocked unconscious. She couldn't imagine that one of them would purposely give out information to the gang.

"That's not possible."

He took her elbow and steered her to the bedroom. "I don't want to think so, but we're not taking any chances. They're making very coordinated moves...just the right ones. It's like they have inside information. I don't have any proof. Just a gut feeling that we need to be extra careful. Don't tell anyone where we're going. We need to keep this between Holmquist, you and me."

A shiver ran up her spine. Her legs started to shake, and she dropped to the edge of the bed. Were there truly only a select few they could trust?

Dylan moved to the door, then glanced back and lowered his voice. "Jenny is on her way. She'll be here any minute."

It seemed like only seconds later when Holmquist answered a knock at the door. A woman with long red hair hurried into the room. She wore a loose-fitting, full-length sundress and paisley shawl, and carried a duffel bag similar to the one Joss had packed.

The woman looked around, then rushed over to hug Joss. "It's so good to see you on your feet."

Joss must have delivered a blank stare, because she reached up and pulled off a wig. Beneath, her blond hair was pulled up and wrapped in a tight bun. "It's me. Jenny."

Joss still didn't recognize her, but the warmth emanating from the woman wrapped around her and she smiled. "Of course." She ducked her head. "Thank you for doing this, Jenny…and for stocking my refrigerator. I can't tell you how much that means to me."

Jenny squeezed her arm. "Don't mention it. You'd do the same for me."

Would she? Everyone around her seemed so convinced that she was a good friend and a good agent. But the facts didn't add up. Why would the gang try to make her look guilty? Did her feelings of guilt revolve around helping her brother in his gang activities?

The cold washed over her in wave after wave. Was she a criminal?

She couldn't believe it—couldn't fathom how she could have betrayed all of these people, who had so much faith and trust in her. It wasn't possible.

"Joss, are you okay?" Jenny grasped her arm.

She swallowed, but couldn't shake the horror. Couldn't seem to break free.

Once again Dylan came to her rescue. He looped his arm around her shoulder and pulled her close. Broke the cold freeze holding her prisoner. She leaned into the comfort of his warm, strong body. He was the only stable thing in her tilting world.

"It's been a rough night. We need to get her settled so she can rest." He explained away the truth, covering for her when she might not deserve it.

"Oh, honey, of course." Jenny grasped her hand. "You've been through so much already. Let's get you changed."

She led Joss into the bedroom, shut the door and pushed her onto the edge of the bed. "You rest while I change."

Soon Jenny exited the bathroom wearing her green border-patrol uniform. Shoulder-length blond hair brushed her shoulders. "Your turn."

She handed Joss the sundress. Jenny was broader and shorter than Joss. The dress didn't fit well, and she exited the bathroom pulling and tugging at the waist.

"Don't worry about the fit. I brought the shawl purposely so we could hide all of that. And I chose the brightest dress I could find. All they'll remember is the bright print."

She turned Joss around. "Let's see if we can get all this gorgeous hair tucked up, underneath that wig."

Jenny twisted Joss's hair, carefully avoiding the swollen knot at the base of her skull. Jenny clicked her tongue. "We'll get them for what they've done to you, Joss. I promise. We'll get them."

But what if Joss was one of them? She closed her eyes as pain shot through her temples. By the time Jenny fit the wig into place, the ache had increased to a dull throb, and things began to blur.

Jenny wrapped the shawl around Joss's shoulders, grabbed the duffel bag and led her out of the bedroom.

Dylan was waiting. "All right. Let's get this going."

He took her bag. Joss grasped the shawl and the skirt of the dress, lifting it slightly. Jenny gave her a hug and Dylan pulled her out the door. They passed the guard and she stumbled a little.

Dylan looked at her. "You okay?"

She nodded.

"I'm going to let go of your arm. You need to walk free, like Jenny did. Can you make it?"

She said yes, but as soon as they left the shelter of the walls and came to the open staircase, her knees began to shake. With trembling fingers, she grasped the stair railing for support.

Who was watching? Did they have guns pinned on her right now?

Sweat beaded and ran along her spine. They crossed the grassy slope to the car. Would her shaky legs make it all the way? When she slid into the seat, a deep sigh escaped her.

"Almost there, Joss. You're doing fine."

She didn't feel fine. She didn't know how anyone watching could have missed her trembling and shaking. But they were safe in the car. Dylan turned on the ignition. Headlights flashed across the grass and bounced against her apartment windows, with their blanket coverings. The last thing she needed was a reminder of that hail of bullets zinging over her head. She closed her eyes.

"We're headed to the police yard. Once we pull into

the gates, we'll switch cars. I want to make sure no one follows us."

The pounding in her head was getting worse. She didn't bother answering.

Dylan reached over the seat, gripped her hand and told her it would be okay. That voice. So deep and secure. She wanted to slip into it, wrap it around her and forget. But she couldn't. She didn't deserve it.

Minutes later they reached the gate into the police station. The barrier clanged behind them as Dylan pulled to a stop. "Okay, Joss. Get out and slip into the back seat of my SUV, then lie down. Stay low and move quickly."

She followed his instructions as best as she could with her head in such agony. In the rear seat, she listened as he slid her bag into the cargo area, started the car and headed out of the driveway. They drove for a long while. She opened her eyes once or twice to watch as Dylan's gaze moved from the rearview mirror to the side one.

"Are we being followed?"

"No. I don't think so."

She closed her eyes again and turned to her side, pressing against the seat. They drove on. Dylan began to sing in his low voice. "I once was lost, but now am found." He continued to sing as the miles sped away. Some of the tension eased from her body, until one thought hit her like the blade of an ax.

If her brother built the tunnels, he would also be the one to tell them how to destroy them.

Her brother… Jason…may have helped them try to kill her.

SIX

A noise woke Joss. She sat straight up in a strange bed.

No, not strange. A bedroom in Dylan's house. As soon as they'd reached Dylan's ranch, she'd simply dropped her duffel and fallen into bed. The bag still sat in the middle of the floor.

The comfortable bed was covered with a well-used, quilted bedspread, in pink and white. Frilly curtains in faded pink covered a wide window and a solid-wood white dresser stood against the opposite wall. Otherwise the room was empty. No pictures nor mementos. Nothing on the walls.

This must have been Beth's room. Once prettily decorated for a beloved daughter and sister...now stripped clean of painful memories.

Like me. Stripped clean of memories. It's the right place for me.

Yesterday's revelation about her brother's potential involvement with the gang, coupled with the fact that he might have had a hand in the explosion that had nearly killed her, sat at the edge of her thoughts. She'd slept from exhaustion, but her sleep was full of dreams. More like nightmares. Images flashed through her mind.

The photo from Dylan's file of Vibora. Only, in the dream, the snake tattoos on his arms came alive, writhing and hissing at her. Caulder laughing, his tone scathing and vicious and aimed at her. Jason hugging her, telling her he loved her and was proud of her. Then with his arm around Maria, he turned from her and walked away.

Some of the dreams seemed so real, she thought they might have happened. Were they nightmares brought on by the photos Dylan had shown her and the terror of last night's attack, or was her memory returning? How could she know for sure?

Persecuted, but not forsaken; cast down, but not destroyed. She had not been abandoned. She could not forget that again. The misty gray wall was beginning to thin. Soon all those frightening images would fall into place. She was sure of it.

With her faith firmly in place again, she pushed the covers off and slid out of bed, anxious to leave the night behind her. The sound of metal banging and quiet conversation pulled her to the window.

Dylan and a stranger were unloading two horses from a trailer. The animals were magnificent. Tall and perfectly formed, with shining coats. A gray Appaloosa and a palomino. Two very distinct and unusual types. Dylan tied both animals to a rail, then helped the man close the trailer. They shook hands and the man drove off. When he was gone, Dylan loosed the horses' reins from the post and walked beyond her sight.

Horses. Her heart leaped upon seeing the beautiful

animals. She knew their color and breed name. Did she know how to ride?

She wasn't sure, but she was about to find out.

She showered in the room's private bath and rummaged through her hastily thrown-together belongings for a pair of jeans and a T-shirt. After slipping into her running shoes, she pulled her damp hair into a ponytail.

She'd barely had time to notice anything about Dylan's home. Now she took a moment to look around at the huge living room. A large river rock fireplace with an oak mantel dominated one side of the space. A brown leather couch and love seat formed two sides of a square, with an opening facing a large TV in the corner. The perfect place to curl up next to Dylan.

In the left corner of the room, several chairs surrounded a long, rectangular oak table. A welcoming, family-sized grouping.

Tucked behind a breakfast bar with an overhanging oak cabinet, a long kitchen sparkled with bright yellow paint and curtains. Open and full of sunshine, like a kitchen should be. A deep sigh slipped out. If she had a home, she'd want it to look exactly like this.

What had Dylan said last night? The house had been in his family for generations. But like the bedroom, the living area was empty of pictures and knickknacks. Nothing provided any hint of the family who had lived here. Just like her apartment. Still, the room itself was welcoming. It spoke of home, a big family and large gatherings. Something that went deep with Joss and felt right.

She didn't know if she'd ever had a home like this.

She only knew she wanted one. She yearned for a place like this and felt more at home than she'd felt in her small apartment. She ran her fingers over the smooth river rock. Closing her eyes, she inhaled, trying to memorize every detail, every sight and smell. An image of what Dylan might look like sprawled on the couch wearing an Arizona Wildcats T-shirt popped into her mind. She forced it out with a vengeance.

Joss had already decided she couldn't cling to him, even in her imagination. Besides, this place wasn't home to Dylan. He didn't want to be here at all. His life centered on his work…on stopping the men who had brought his life here to an end. The death of his beloved sister had destroyed everything. Now that Joss had seen this wonderful place, Dylan's desire to fight drug trafficking meant more to her. If she'd had a home like this and lost it, she might be as driven.

At least that was how she felt now. This place—the heritage it represented, its potential as a home and the man in it—seemed like a dream worth having. She was pretty certain it was a dream the "pre-accident Joss" did not have. Everything had changed for her but nothing had changed for Dylan.

She couldn't afford to forget that again.

Stepping outside, Joss saw a small patch of grass covering a square in front of the sprawling brick ranch house. A gravel road led to the side. Directly in front, huge cottonwood trees reached high into the sky—and had for generations. Their size attested to that. They ruled over the yard and the empty field on the other side.

Beyond those massive monarchs, the field burst with

natural grasses and spiny yuccas. Farther on, a dark ribbon of tall cottonwoods wound away, into the distance, marking the path of water. The San Pedro River. Dylan had said his home was close to it.

The neigh of a horse dragged her attention away from the land blanketed in green from the monsoon rains. Following the gravel road, she hurried around the house. Not far away, a large barn stood in serious need of a coat of paint. The wide doors opened themselves to the sunshine.

Joss stepped inside. The Appaloosa and palomino were tied outside the closest stalls. Dylan used long, firm strokes to brush the coat of the Appaloosa.

Gravel crunched beneath her feet as she stepped forward.

"About time you woke. The day is wasting away."

Joss made a sound. "What am I going to do today that's so important?"

Dylan shook his head. "You're going to put everything behind you and relax. I can't think of a better way to do that than to spend time with these guys."

He spoke without turning. He wore a weathered tan cowboy hat. His dark curling hair peeked out around the edges. The hat looked natural, like it belonged on his head, and he brushed the horse's coat with comfortable familiarity.

Joss walked close, awestruck by the amazing animals. They seemed so much larger up close. They stood far above her head. She reached a hand up to touch the palomino's shiny coat, but he shivered.

She jerked back and clutched her hands together as she slid a glance at Dylan. He seemed not to notice.

"Are they yours?"

"Yeah. They stay with Hank Martin, my neighbor on the next ranch. He takes care of them. I asked him to bring them over, and his wife sent some groceries and a casserole. They're good neighbors." He paused to run his bare hand along the Appaloosa's coat. "I should have sold these horses to him a long time ago, but…"

He didn't finish. A fly landed on the palomino's flank and he shivered again. Joss stepped farther back.

Dylan paused to look sideways at her. "Do you ride?"

She bit her lip. "I don't think so. I might be a little afraid. They're so big."

"Yep. They are. But they're the best kind of friend." He patted the Appaloosa. "I didn't realize how much I missed them."

He strode to a nearby bench and grabbed a rubber brush. "He needs to be curried. Brush against the grain like this."

He didn't give her a chance to hesitate or say no. He put the brush in her hand and cupped it with his own. It was warm and big and covered her hand completely. With his other, he gripped her shoulder and turned her to face the palomino. Then he stepped close behind her—so close, she could smell him.

Soap and damp cotton. A good, clean smell. He placed her hand with the brush on the horse, then took her other hand and set it a few inches away. The horse jerked reflexively and she wanted to pull away, but Dylan's hand on hers, and his arms around her, kept her in place. Soft breath teased the hair close to the back of her neck, and shivers tripped up her spine.

Beneath her fingertips the horse's coat was smooth. The muscles beneath rippled and her hands slid over him like silk.

"They like to be touched. It comforts them." Dylan's voice was low and gentle. "Like people."

If she turned, his lips would only be inches away. What would it be like to kiss Dylan? To feel his warm lips on hers? Would it be as comforting as his touch? Or would it make her tingle and spin like now?

"Talk to them. They like to hear your voice."

Like she liked to hear his? The sound of it, low and rumbling, made her knees weak, as if she could melt right into him.

The palomino chose that moment to shift, stepped sideways into Joss and she jerked back, right against Dylan. His hand came around her waist, steadying her, and pulling her close for one breathtaking moment. She pressed her head to the curve of his neck and closed her eyes. He held her tight, close and safe for a moment. Then he released her and moved away.

"I think you've got the picture." His voice rasped a little.

Joss looked at him. Dylan didn't glance her way or pause, but he'd felt the elemental pull. He acted as if nothing had happened. Or that he didn't feel what she did. But it was a lie. He felt it.

In her condition she couldn't lie or pretend. Her entire life had become one of cold, hard truth. That's all she knew for sure. And the truth was, the feelings that

washed between them were real. Not fiery and passionate, but deep and still. Like a continuous river current.
Steady. Strong. They were the kind of bonds that created a lifetime of love. The feelings were new, barely
there, like cool water in the hot August sun. But they
were as real as the warm flesh of the horse's flank beneath her fingertips.

And just as impossible as before. Dylan was focused.
Driven, like Holmquist said. Now that she'd seen his
home, she understood more. He'd lost a wonderful
family life and a home, but because of his loss, he'd
become a legend in law enforcement circles. He'd cut
a wide swath through criminal gangs, while she…she
was more than likely guilty. Of what she didn't know,
couldn't remember. But since she'd left the hospital,
she'd learned to trust her feelings. They were strong
and certain, and they told her she was guilty. She'd done
something wrong. That was the only feeling that had not
left her since her awakening. And because of the guilt,
of that wrongdoing, she had no place beside Dylan.

Ever.

They worked side by side. Dylan hummed, trying to
distract himself from Joss's closeness, but it didn't work.
He was acutely aware of her every movement. The light
summery scent of cucumbers. How she touched the
horse, with her graceful fingers stroking it as she might
a cherished treasure. Long white fingers, softly rounded
nails—they looked as if they should be stroking piano
keys, not the shiny gold coat of a horse.

Yet another discordant image. Joss was one giant

puzzle. Mixed images. Lost memories. Brave but terrified. Strong but helpless. She was different from his "hotshot," the woman he'd met weeks ago, but the same in many ways…the ones that counted. He knew she was hiding something…still, she had innocent ways.

But there was nothing innocent about the things she brought to life inside him. She made him yearn for things he couldn't have, had turned his back on years ago. Those thoughts were pointless and painful, and they needed to stop. Right now. He needed to get on track, but he couldn't take his gaze off the sight of her slender, graceful hands as they smoothed over Goldie's flank.

His jaw clenched and he brushed a little too vigorously. Patches neighed softly and shifted. Gritting his teeth, he patted the animal's side. "Sorry, fella."

He needed a distraction.

"His name is Patches. And this one—" he pointed to Joss's horse "—is Goldie."

"Patches to match the gray spots."

"Yep. Not very original, but my sister was only eight when she named them and they were ponies."

"They were her horses? Both of them?"

A tactical error. The tenderness in her voice brought back all the feelings he was trying hard to put away. Her knowing tone brought an edge to his voice. "Yes. She raised them from colts. She was good. Could have been a horse trainer if drugs hadn't killed her." He intended his tone to be harsh…like the truth.

"I see why you couldn't get rid of them."

Did she see…really see? Did she know what it was

like to get a phone call in the middle of the night? To hear your mother sobbing in the background. Your father's broken voice calling you home. Did she know what it was like to look down on the battered, pale, dead body of a little sister he could still see climbing onto the fence so she could reach Patches?

Joss watched him with eyes like the cloudy gray sky outside. The gaze was open but troubled. The empathy in those beautiful eyes told him yes, she did understand that kind of pain. That's why she didn't want to remember.

He didn't want to remember either. After tossing the brush to the bench, he wiped his hands down his pant legs. "Let's go for a ride."

Her pink lips parted. "I don't think I know how."

"I'll teach you. Besides, these guys are getting older. They're over fifteen now, so not quite as rambunctious as they used to be. Let's get out of here."

His tone brooked no argument. Beth's saddles rested on the stands in the same spot where their father had placed them years ago. The leather was dry and brittle, but they would do for a quick lesson. He pulled the first one off and slid it onto Goldie's back. All the while he kept up a steady monologue, pretending he was teaching Joss how to cinch up a horse, but really just drowning out his own thoughts.

He led the horses to the corral behind the barn. Joss climbed the fence in the same spot Beth had used to mount the horses. He showed Joss how to sit, to brace her feet slightly to break the bounce. She might not know how to ride, but she was a natural, catching on even as Dylan talked.

At last they were ready. He edged open the gate and

they headed to the river, with Joss ahead of him, on Goldie. For a long while he watched her closely, making sure she was in control. When she reached down, stroked Goldie's neck and murmured, "Good boy," he knew it was safe to relax a little.

He sat straighter in the saddle and looked around. The land hadn't changed much. The monsoons had brought a green covering to barren fields that had once been filled with hay and alfalfa for his father's cattle. Fortunately the thoughts that usually came with those memories stayed at bay.

He didn't see images of the past. Instead he studied the wild grasses gleaming gold in spots where the cloudy sky let the sun through.

He let the clean air burn away all of the haunting images and all thoughts, until all that remained was the smell of the horses and the woman ahead of him, her body moving with the palomino, hair swaying, bobbing with a different rhythm. That ponytail made him smile.

He brought her to the ranch for her safety, but seeing her here pleased him in ways he'd never imagined... the slight smile wavering over her lips, those sparkling gray eyes, her delight in the animals. The ranch was isolated, so the gang would never guess that she was here, but more than any other reason, he felt this place would be good for her. Some gut feeling told him she'd find healing here.

He didn't know why he felt that way...especially since he'd spent eight years avoiding this place like the plague. He only knew it was right for her.

Joss slowed to a stop along the bank of the river. She

held the reins tightly in her hand, almost as if she were afraid Goldie would tumble down the steep, dirt-filled bank to the muddy water below.

"Someone told me the San Pedro was dry. That looks pretty full of water to me."

"It's monsoon season. All the washes around here feed into the river. It's probably ten feet deep during the summer rains. In the dry season, it'll trickle to nothing. But it never stops flowing. The waters simply sink beneath the ground and bubble up in other places."

"You know this river…this place well."

"Like the back of my hand."

He glanced toward the ranch house. "Do you want to head in?"

"Do you?"

He shook his head. "Not yet. I'd like to go a little way along the river." His hand shot to his hip, where his Glock rested in its holster, then to the cell phone hooked to the belt. Both were safely in place, so they could go on. But one thing needed fixing.

"You need this." After lifting his hat, he settled it on her head. It slid down almost to her ears, but it shaded the white skin of her cheeks. That was important. Joss's soft skin was far too pretty to turn an angry red.

She smiled and tilted the hat slightly. "Does it look right?"

Better than right. It looked perfect. Her dark ponytail hanging down the back, the white T-shirt and blue jeans against Goldie's flank. She hadn't stopped smiling since she'd climbed onto Goldie. She looked like a natural, a dream…one that could never come true.

Swallowing hard, he tamped down his longing and said, "You look fine." Then he gave Patches a gentle kick, reined around Goldie and headed upriver.

The trail wove beside the bank. The roar of rushing water soothed the tension in his shoulders. For the first time in days, he allowed them to relax. The cottonwood leaves whispered a soft welcome. They brought another smile to his lips.

"You're enjoying this very much, aren't you?"

He turned, surprised to find Joss's gaze fixed on him. "I suppose I am. Horses always make me happy."

"Are you sure it's the horses?"

Afraid of where her thoughts were going, he fixed his gaze on her. "What does that mean?"

She gave a little shake of her head. Her dark ponytail got caught on her shoulder. He wanted to reach over and smooth it back.

"I don't know. It's just…well, for someone who didn't want to come back here, you seem to like it a lot."

He rested one hand on his thigh as Patches skirted a bump in the path with a little hop. "I came here for you. I knew this place would be good for you."

"Right."

He glanced over. The sarcasm in her tone was unmistakable, and another kind of smile settled on her lips. The kind that said she knew better.

She was right. He had enjoyed being home. The land. The horses. Even his old friend Hank sparked something to life inside him…something he'd thought was dead a long time ago.

"I never said I didn't like it." He pulled Patches to

a stop and studied the brown water as it surged on its path. "The memories drove me away."

"Are they gone now?"

He shook his head. "Never. They'll never go away."

There it was. The reason he could never be content here. He had a job to do. A purpose. He couldn't lose sight of that. He kicked Patches into motion. The animal gave a little jump and hurried ahead, leaving Joss behind. She only caught up when he slowed. The pleasure in the ride was gone, and he stopped, waiting for her so they could turn around.

She rode up and raised a hand to hold the hat in place as a breeze picked up. "You know, it's kind of sad."

Frowning, he turned Patches around to face her. "What?"

"I'm desperate to remember and you want to forget."

Dark brows framed those wide gray eyes. There was nothing open about them now. They were troubled and thunderous, like the clouds gathering overhead. The sight of them made the air electric, like a brewing storm. But no matter how intense her emotions seemed, her words were false.

"You're wrong. I don't want to forget. I'll never forget what happened to Beth." Tugging on his horse's reins, he pulled around Goldie and headed to the ranch. Patches picked up the pace, leaving Joss behind again.

She caught up quickly this time—too quickly. "Did you ever think that maybe those memories don't go away because they are the only ones you have?"

Dylan sighed, his pleasure in the ride completely gone now. "What's that supposed to mean?"

"This is your home. A place where, from what I've seen, you belong. But you don't want to be here. Too many bad memories. Maybe if you made new ones… good ones…the others would go away."

His irritation hardened and he squinted as thunder rumbled in the distance. "Is that what you are doing? Making all new memories and forgetting the old ones?"

"I don't know what you mean."

"I've seen how every time you get close to remembering something valuable to us, it creates some kind of emotional struggle. Your headaches return not long after that."

Her lips parted and she was silent for a time, long enough for Dylan to regret his hastily spoken words.

At last she said, "I hadn't noticed, but you may be right. Maybe I don't want to remember because the truth is I feel guilty."

Thunder rumbled again, closer this time. The afternoon shower was about to hit, and when it did, it would come in a deluge. The horses were already skittish and so was Joss. She hated storms and kept shooting a nervous glance upwards. But maybe this was what she needed, this explosive confrontation of the truth. Maybe it would jostle her memory.

He pulled Patches to a halt and turned in the saddle to face her. "Maybe you feel guilty because you were covering up your brother's gang activities."

"I don't think so. It's not that."

Frustration rolled like a hard ball in his stomach as the horse continued its trot. "You don't remember but you can say it's not that. Maybe the truth is you don't want to face the fact that the brother you love so much abandoned you to Vibora's vengeance."

She halted Goldie and stared at him.

"That's not true. Jason would never abandon me."

He pulled the horse to an abrupt halt. "How can you say that so confidently? Did you remember something?"

She shook her head. "No, it just doesn't...feel right."

The horses shifted between them, sensing their tension and nervous about the oncoming storm.

"Feelings." Dylan's tone was more dismissive than he'd intended.

"Don't say it like that. Like my feelings have no meaning."

"I'm not belittling your emotions."

"You better not be. Your whole life is built around a feeling of guilt over Beth's death."

Shock waves surged over Dylan. He stared at Joss for a long while, not quite believing the words that had come out of her mouth. "My life is not about guilt. It's about stopping men who need to be stopped."

She made a small dismissive sound and shook her head. "That's what you tell yourself. But believe me, if I had all of this..." She gestured around to the land. "If this were mine, I'd find a way to fight crime and stay where I belonged. Admit it, Dylan, the reason you have no joy, no life, is because subconsciously you think you don't deserve it. You think it's your fault Beth died."

Anger flamed through Dylan and he retaliated. "And you feel guilty because you knew Jason was a gang member."

She shook her head, blindly, angrily, but Dylan didn't

back down. "You knew he had something to do with those tunnels, but you didn't report him. That's why you don't want to remember."

"No! I didn't know! I'm sure of it. He kept it from me, always tried to protect me. But I know he never would have been involved with the gang if he didn't leave school to take care of me! It's all because of me!"

Her tone of assurance shocked both of them, and there was a moment of stunned silence.

Thunder cracked over their heads and the clouds split open. Goldie jumped and shied away. Patches skittered to the side. Joss fumbled with the reins and Dylan feared Goldie would bolt. Joss feared storms. She might panic too. But just when he thought the horse might break, she leaned on Goldie's neck, laid her cheek flat on his shivering coat and wrapped her arms around him, holding on for life. The gesture seemed to settle the horse. He shivered once, then stood stock-still as Joss held on, comforting him and herself with nearness.

Dylan brought Patches closer. The rain, coming down like buckets of water, had already soaked Joss's hair. The long ponytail was plastered to her T-shirt. Was that rain on her cheeks…or tears? Probably both. But the sight of her clinging to the animal brought an unwanted wave of tenderness over him.

He never meant to make her cry. He brought her here to help her heal, not to cause her more pain.

Water poured down his face and dripped off the tip of his nose, blurring the image in front of him. Soaked and weary from his own seesawing emotions, he kicked

Patches into motion. Reaching across, he gave Goldie's reins a tug. "Come on. Let's get out of the rain."

They left the riverbank and crossed the field. All the while Dylan's conscience ate at him. Was Joss right? In his heart of hearts, did he feel he had no right to a life of happiness?

No. He had a God-given mission to stop drug traffic wherever he could. His successes, which far exceeded his failures, assured him that he was on the right path. The feelings and ideas Joss brought to life inside him were distractions. His job was to focus, to clear away the debris and emotions blocking the return of her memory. That was all.

The rain pelted them so hard, it felt like little needles. Joss sagged on her horse like a woman in pain. Dylan made an angry sound, disgusted with himself for allowing the distraction of a ride to get in the way of Joss's recovery. If she suffered a setback…

Finally the wide-open doors of the barn appeared. Dylan led the way inside. The cool, dark interior raised goose bumps on his wet skin. Joss would probably feel the chill more.

He tied off Patches and looked to her. Joss hadn't moved. She sat slumped on Goldie, staring off into the distance…trembling. The storm and his harsh words, true or not, had gotten to her.

He secured Goldie's reins, then reached for Joss. She tumbled into his arms, trusting completely that he could carry her weight. That trust tore a layer of his resistance somewhere inside him.

Did he deserve that trust when his main objective

was to solve his case regardless of how the outcome affected Joss? Suddenly his determination seemed like a betrayal. Didn't she deserve more? Wasn't she worth it?

Her arms looped around his neck as his hands held her waist rock steady and close to his body. Her chin tilted up and she looked at him with eyes completely honest and open.

His resolve crumbled. Joss was more than a distraction. She was a dream he could never have. But didn't he deserve one sweet kiss to remember? One stolen moment to carry him through the rest of his life?

He lowered his head and pressed his lips to hers.

SEVEN

Joss's lips tingled where Dylan's touched hers. It was an incredible sensation that made her head spin. But his warm, strong hands around her waist kept her anchored. Grounded. Real. His lips parted slightly and he tilted his head, kissing her breathless.

Real and safe. Needed and never alone. His kiss created wonderful emotions inside her. Amazing feelings that she'd wanted from the moment his deep, safe voice had rumbled into the darkness of her coma. She'd wanted him from that first second…maybe even longer. His kiss answered a need inside her that stretched further back than her accident. Maybe from forever.

A sense of belonging…of togetherness.

He'd said they were just friends before, but he meant more to her. Somehow she felt that truth. He might not feel the same, but Joss knew in her heart of hearts that Dylan had been special to her long before now. She'd wanted more, needed this even before the accident. Being in his arms, their lips together, answered a deep, deep need. She knew it as surely as she felt his strong hands, holding her steady and close.

Thunder clapped over their heads and Goldie shuffled, bumping against them. Dylan broke the kiss but held her close, staring into her eyes. "I need to take care of these horses."

She nodded, not willing for the moment to end. But a cool breeze swept into the barn and she shivered. Dylan held her in place and stepped back, a whole space away. "You should go in and take a hot shower. We don't need for you to get sick after we've worked so hard to get you well."

She nodded again, not speaking, hoping to hang on to the wonderful feelings flowing through her. But shivers tripped over her and she knew Dylan was right. She needed to get warm.

Inside, she went straight to the shower. Wrapped in warm sweats and socks, she combed out her hair and her stomach rumbled. She couldn't remember the last time she'd eaten. She hurried into the living room, with her tummy grumbling all the way.

Dylan sat at the table, in front of the big picture window. Behind him, rain slid down the dining room glass in sheets. Thunder boomed outside. The clean, fresh scent of rain and green things flowed through the screen door with the breeze. For the first time in... forever, the sound of a storm didn't make her uncomfortable. She liked it...here.

Dylan had showered too. He wore a clean white T-shirt and jeans. She might not have known it before, might not have worked hard to accomplish this goal, but this good man seated at the kitchen table was what she wanted. What she suspected she'd secretly yearned for all of her life. To belong to someone. To know he belonged to her forever. It touched a need so overwhelming, it was all she could do not to run across the room, wrap her arms around him and kiss him again.

She suspected he would not appreciate the gesture, so she stood where she was, capturing the sight of him, the smell of the rain…even the thunder. She wanted to remember it long after it was over.

Dylan seemed to sense her presence. He looked up and shifted uncomfortably. "Would you like something to eat?"

The moment broken, Joss said, "I'd love it."

"Hank's wife sent over her specialty…meatloaf with Hatch chilies. Sit and I'll heat some up for you. I had a plate while you were in the shower. I also checked in on Henderson. He's doing well." He paused. "When you're finished, we need to talk about what you remember."

She finished the delicious meatloaf quickly, then pushed her plate away. Leaning forward, with her chin on the heel of her hand, she stared at Dylan as he worked on the files spread out in front of him.

After a long while he said, "You need to stop looking at me like that."

"Like what?"

"Like you want me to kiss you again."

"I do."

He sighed. "Joss…"

"Don't, Dylan. You don't need to say another word. I know there can never be anything between us. You

have your work, more of a mission than work. And I…"
She had her guilt over Jason.

She licked her dry lips. "What I said out there in the
storm was true. I remembered my feelings about Jason,
and this time there was a memory to go with it."

"What memory?"

"I was sitting outside my brother's apartment, feeling as if it was all my fault. I didn't know he'd left town,
but I suspected he was involved with the gang. I felt responsible because he'd given up the career he loved to
take care of me."

Dylan's features tightened. Because he didn't believe
her, or because what she'd said outside was too close to
the truth about his own motives?

She couldn't tell. He'd made himself unreadable…
drawn a line in the sand and refused to let her cross
over. He wouldn't share himself or allow her to shelter in the peace of his safety anymore. That was over.

She was alone…again. Pain filled her so intensely,
it clutched at her chest. She closed her eyes and waited
for the emptiness to wash over her.

But it didn't come. Not this time.

*Persecuted, but not forsaken; cast down, but not
destroyed.*

She wasn't alone. Dylan hadn't betrayed her. She'd
betrayed herself, fallen into an old trap by trying to
place a man, a human, in the place created for God.
Only He could fill that hole. Only He could satisfy a
soul thirsting with a need so great that it would overwhelm any mortal human.

It was unfair to expect anyone else to take that place.

People would fail. They would die like her parents or make mistakes like her brother and Dylan, but God would never fail her.

After pulling a clean piece of paper from Dylan's pile, she grabbed a pencil and wrote the scripture down.

"What's this?" Dylan pulled it toward him.

"A scripture I remember."

He froze. "You remember a scripture?"

"It came to me after the gang destroyed my apartment. It keeps coming back to me. It's given me strength."

He read it out loud, then pushed the paper to her. "By all means, keep reading it. Maybe it will stir other memories."

She closed her eyes and whispered the words again. Amazingly, another image appeared. Blurry at first. Shrouded in the gray mist of her memory loss. But she was sure it was real; she felt, heard and tasted it. Her hands were tied. But a voice came loud and clear. A man's voice. He demanded she open her eyes.

The man slapped her. She tasted blood in her mouth and finally was able to open her eyes and look at him. He stared at her. Slicked hair. Man-bun.

Vibora.

"I want you awake," he said. "I want you to feel every second as the clock ticks..."

She gasped and her eyes flew open.

Dylan dropped his pen. "It worked?"

Silent, startled and filled with wonder, she stared at him.

Dylan's breath caught. "You remembered something important."

Joss nodded slowly. "Vibora, in my face, screaming at me. Demanding I tell him where Jason and Maria had gone."

Dylan inhaled, slow and steady. A half smile slipped over his lips. Was it because he was as relieved as she was? She couldn't tell. The wall he'd built between them was thick, like the gray mist of her memory loss.

"You remember Vibora questioning you, trying to find out where your brother and Maria were hiding."

She gave a quick nod of her head. Clarity nipped at the edges of her mind and gave her disjointed images. And sensations—pain, fear, the smell of something dank and dirty. She closed her eyes, hoping memories would connect with the sensations. She gasped when an image appeared.

"It was dark. We were in the tunnel. Caulder was there too. And that other man...the one you call Snake Man. Vibora was in my face, striking me. He told me to wake up. He wanted me to know what was happening, so I'd suffer every minute until the explosion."

Excitement lifted his features. "So they kidnapped you? You can testify to that?"

"Absolutely. But I don't know how I ended up in the tunnel."

"Dr. Hull said it's normal. Victims of accidents often forget the moments leading up to it or the event itself. That's the brain's way of forgetting and allowing itself to heal."

"I remember driving on the highway and pulling

into a parking lot of a large building. I think it was the abandoned storage place our team had under surveillance. After that I don't remember anything until waking up in the tunnel. But they were holding me against my will. I know that. That's clear in my mind."

"This is the break I've been hoping for, Joss. Now that we know you were kidnapped, we can charge Vibora and Caulder. We have them, Joss!" He reached for her, as if he were going to pull her into his arms. At the last minute he pulled back, but not before Joss saw the look in his eyes.

He could deny it but he wanted her as much as she wanted him. Unfortunately his determination, the guilt that drove him, was stronger than both of them.

His features hardened and he shifted in his chair. "Do you remember anything else? Any other gang members?"

"Show me the pictures again."

She studied them for a while and picked out three more. "I was sitting outside of Jason's apartment. He must have left town already but I didn't know it. I was worried sick and hoping he'd show up any minute. Then three men walked out." She pointed. "These three. I'm pretty sure I followed them."

"Where did they go? Do you recognize any places? Maybe we can piece together a possible location."

She squeezed her eyes shut tightly. "A freeway. I remember a sign... Nogales! I was on the road to Nogales."

Dylan frowned. "Were they leading you to the safe house or the tunnel?"

Joss shook her head. "I don't know. The last thing I

remember before waking up in the tunnel is that freeway sign."

"Why didn't you call for backup?"

"I'm not sure. I think… I don't know." She shook her head again. "I don't know my reasoning, just the feeling that I needed to protect my brother."

"From us or the gang?"

"I don't remember. Maybe both."

Dylan studied her. "You remember the car you followed?"

"Yes. The Toyota truck you described." She frowned. "But the pieces don't fit together. If they kidnapped me, why did they try to kill me before I revealed Jason's location?"

"You were pretty beat up, Joss. I think they worked you over and found out you didn't know anything."

"If they know that, what was the point of trying to frame me with the heroin, and why are they still trying to kill me?"

Dylan's lips thinned. "Maybe to throw us off and stall for time."

"Stall for time? Why?"

Dylan's features were grim. "To give Jason time to find out they had you. We've seen how Vibora works. He's a vicious killer. He's also overconfident. He thinks he'll get your brother eventually, and he takes pleasure in frightening his victims. Your death might have been meant as a warning. To let your brother and Maria know he's coming after them and it won't be pretty when he finds them."

She stared at Dylan. "We can't let them fall into his hands."

Reaching across the space, he ran a finger along her cheek. "Right now your brother is in hiding. We can't let Vibora get his hands on you or Lena Jones."

She gripped his hand. "You're worried about the transfer in the morning."

"Vibora has known every move we've made so far. I'm sure they'll be waiting for us."

"What can you do?"

He was silent for a long moment. "We need to move Lena's transfer up. Now. Tonight. They won't be expecting it."

She agreed with a firm nod. "You need to go, Dylan."

"I can't leave you alone."

"Call Holmquist. I trust him completely."

He agreed. "I'll do it right now and get the ball rolling."

She listened to his one-sided conversation as he filled Holmquist in on all that had happened. Then he spoke Chekowski's name. At last Dylan said, "I don't like it, but I guess we don't have any choice."

He hung up. "There's been an incident near the border. Holmquist is there. He won't get here in time, but he'll head over here as soon as he can. In the meantime he's calling Chekowski."

She shrugged. "The gang shot at him, knocked him unconscious at my apartment. He's one of us. We can trust him."

Dylan hesitated.

She squeezed his hand again. "You have to go. You

can't let Vibora get his hands on Lena and her little boy. I'll be fine until Chekowski arrives."

She sounded so firm and certain.

Please, Lord. Let it be true.

EIGHT

Joss sat for a long while after Dylan left, staring at the photos and notes. No new memories came to her, but her feelings grew stronger. Jason had loved his studies and his school. Taking the job in the mechanic shop had been a necessity, not a pleasure. She'd lived with the knowledge that he'd given up his dreams, jumped in to take care of her without a thought. Jason had sacrificed so much for her, left his studies so she could finish years of schooling. He was so kindhearted, so willing to help those he loved…anyone in need. She could easily see how he would have agreed to help Maria escape.

She rose from the table and went to the fridge. It was dusk, way past dinner, and she was hungry. The meatloaf from Hank's wife filled the fridge with a tantalizing smell, so she put a plate of it in the microwave. When the food was hot, she pulled it out, opened the back door and leaned against the jamb to eat the meatloaf.

The sinking sun in the west was beautiful…a gigantic fireball casting an orange light through the clouds left over from the storm. They too looked like they were on fire. The whole sky was aflame.

The evening air was still hot. Her skin tingled from the transition of the cold air-conditioning to the heat, but still it felt good, comfortable, like she'd done it many times before. She was settling into her life again.

She finished eating and closed the door. Right after she placed the dishes in the sink and began to wash them, she heard a car engine grumble and gravel crunch.

Chekowski was here. Wiping her hands on a kitchen towel, she hurried to the front door. Before she could reach it, the handle moved back and forth, almost without a sound. She halted in her footsteps.

Why was Chekowski trying the handle? Why didn't he knock or call out her name? His stealthy behavior made her pulse pound. Maybe it wasn't Chekowski!

She rushed to the door as silently as possible and flattened herself against the wall. The handle didn't budge, so a heavy tread crossed the wooden porch, toward the large picture window in front of the dining room table. A shadow fell across the table…a big, bulky shadow that somehow looked familiar.

Definitely Chekowski. She recognized his shadow from the day they had been ambushed. But why was he skulking around? Why didn't he make himself known? It was almost as if he were trying to catch her unaware, as if he were expecting her to give him trouble.

Something wasn't right. The shadow moved around the corner, toward the back door.

Did she lock it?

She stared at the door. If she'd forgotten to flip the lock, he'd get inside.

Was she being paranoid? Hadn't he helped to defend her at her brother's apartment?

Until she knew what was behind his stealthy behavior, she wasn't ready to face him. She needed to keep out of sight until she could figure out why her senses were jangling like live wires.

But where could she hide? Her mind raced over the rooms of the house. There were no secret corners or locked closets.

The barn. Maybe she could make it to the barn.

As quietly as possible, she flipped the old-fashioned lock on the front door and turned the handle. It opened without a sound. Sliding out, she closed it behind her. Still no sound.

She ran across the porch, on tiptoes, and down the steps. Even the gravel seemed to cooperate and hardly made a whisper as she ran to the barn.

The horses nickered when they saw her. She glanced over her shoulder. The kitchen door must have been unlocked, because there was still no sign of Chekowski. He had to be inside, searching the house, and still hadn't called out for her. What was his game?

Inside the barn a ladder led to a small alcove where bales of hay were stacked three high. She might be able to squeeze between the wall and the stack.

She scurried up the ladder, feeling her heart pounding. The hay smelled dusty and moldy. The bales must have been stacked when Dylan's family lived on the ranch. The rotting smell made her nose tickle and she sneezed.

Freezing, she listened for the sound of footsteps outside the barn.

Hearing nothing, she scooted along the outer edge of the loft. Her foot slipped. She grabbed at the top bale. The loose hay gave way. Joss nearly tipped over the edge of the eight-foot drop. Beneath her the horses shifted nervously and banged against their stalls.

At last the top bale snagged and held. Joss wavered but finally got her balance. Closing her eyes, she leaned against the pile and sighed in relief.

The front door of the house opened, jolting her into action again. She wiggled between the wall and the bales. Dust and pieces of straw filtered to the ground, silhouetted in the last streams of daylight. The horses shifted again.

If she hoped to stay hidden, she needed to stop moving and creating dust.

The bottom bale was all the way against the wall. No way could she make room for her feet. But the second bale was inches away from the wall. Flattening herself, she slid into the slight opening. There was enough room for her to crouch.

Gravel crunched outside. Chekowski was coming. Joss held her breath and closed her eyes.

Please, God. Don't let more straw fall. If it does, he'll look up and see my hiding place.

Seconds of painful silence passed. Joss had to release her breath in a slow, controlled whisper. Her thighs burned from crouching. Blood pounded in her ears. It was all she could do not to gasp. Her nose tickled and she felt a sneeze coming on. She pressed her fingers to her nose and squeezed.

The door opened. She heard footsteps cross the floor. The horses shuffled again. Why was Chekowski so silent? His furtive manner hadn't changed, and her nerves still danced like loose wires.

Had he seen her? Was he even now climbing the ladder, preparing to poke over the top and order her out?

Clothing rustled. Then the muffled sound of a phone ringing. A voice on the other end answered.

"Yeah, it's me. I'm here but there's no sign of her." She recognized Chekowski's low rumble. Was he contacting Holmquist or Dylan? Should she step out and let him know she was all right?

"Yeah, yeah. I'm sure it's the right place. But it's deserted. No one's here."

The voice on the other end of the phone said something in response, but Joss couldn't make out the words.

"I'm telling you, she's not here. I've searched everywhere…even the barn. Maybe she got scared and took off."

Garbled words on the other end. "How do I know where she went?"

Joss was about to call out, to let him know she was all right. His next words stopped her cold.

"Of course I was careful. I came in silently, because I wanted to get a jump on her. For all I know she has a weapon now and knows how to use it. I'm not gonna get myself killed for you."

More garbled yelling from the phone.

"I don't have to take that. She's not where Holmquist said she'd be, so I'm heading back. If you don't like it...too bad."

Cold washed through her.

Chekowski cursed. "Don't threaten me, you little..."

He was interrupted by shouting from the other end of the phone.

"I've done my part. You want more from me, you're gonna have to come up with more money." He punched the phone and cut off the furious-sounding voice.

Chekowski was the traitor. The gang had been paying him money to keep them informed.

Shocked, Joss's fingers slipped from her nose. Immediately a sneeze escaped, exploded across the silent barn.

"What the...?"

Caught! She had to move, do something.

Placing her back against the wall, she pushed the bale. The outer, molded edges of the bale fell away in a dusty flow. But thankfully the center had more substance. She shoved hard against the bulk.

It flew down. Chekowski cried out and raised an arm to block the remnants of the hay bale. But it hit his head, knocking him to the ground.

Move! Go now!

Joss leaped to her feet and clambered down the ladder. She slipped. Her feet missed the final two rungs. Splinters slid into her hands as she gripped the sides of the wooden ladder, but she managed to keep her feet as she hit the ground.

Unfortunately the hay had only deterred Chekowski for a moment. He rose. Hatless and covered in hay, he looked like a nightmarish scarecrow rising from the straw-scattered floor. He'd lost his gun somewhere in the pile.

She spun for the door. Bellowing his rage, Chekowski lunged and grasped her ankle. She landed flat on her chest and gasped, the wind knocked out of her.

Catching her breath, she glanced over her shoulder. He'd risen to his feet, still gripping her ankle with both hands while he dragged his foot through the hay, searching for his dropped weapon.

She turned over, facedown, and clawed at the ground, trying to get away, but Chekowski was too strong. He hauled her backward. If he found his gun...

Looking over her shoulder again, she spied the horses' bridles looped on the corral. If she could reach them...

After rolling to her right side, she pushed herself up and twisted her body at the same time. Her loose leg swung high and wide. Her foot struck Chekowski on the jaw with a glancing blow, just enough for him to momentarily release her other ankle. She squirmed sideways to the corral and jerked one of the bridles down.

Chekowski recovered quickly and snatched at her again, but Joss swung the bridle around like a whip. The end with the metal bit struck him on the side of the head, and he dropped like a sack of cement...straight onto her legs.

Bending her knees, she squirmed out from beneath his heavy body and kicked free. Then she crawled to his side and secured his hands with his own handcuffs. On her knees, Joss slid her hands through the hay, searching for the gun.

She heard running feet. Did Chekowski have an accomplice?

Her fingers latched on to the cool metal. She grasped it and spun, landing flat on her bottom, with her legs splayed out in front of her and the weapon pointed at the barn door.

It creaked open slowly. Joss's heart pounded. Holmquist peeked out from the edge.

"Joss! What...?"

She sagged and dropped the gun. He ran toward her and helped her to her feet. She threw her arms around him.

"Are you hurt?"

"No. I'm all right."

"What's going on?"

"Chekowski is the leak. The gang is paying him for information." She shook her head. "I should have remembered, seen the connection. The day we left my apartment, Chekowski said he was texting his supervisor to keep him informed. But later he used the radio on his shoulder to call for backup."

"Standard procedure on a special assignment like that, Joss."

He missed the point and she shook her head. "No, not standard. Why did he text his supervisor when he could have used the radio?"

Holmquist's face reflected his understanding. "Of course. He didn't text his supervisor. He contacted the gang so they could be waiting to ambush you at your brother's apartment."

"And he knows that Dylan moved up Lena Jones's transfer to tonight. You have to warn them."

Holmquist reached for his phone, then paused. "If Chekowski knows everything, then the gang knows your location. We have to get you away from here."

She shook her head. "I was hiding. I heard him speak to someone from the gang and tell them I wasn't here. My location is safe for now. Call Dylan. Warn him. The gang knows about the transfer."

Lights flashed past Dylan on the freeway. He was only twenty minutes out of Tucson. He'd contacted Gonzalez and told him to prep Lena Jones but not to inform the team.

Everything was in place. He'd coordinated with a new team. This one came from Phoenix. They were on their way to the Tucson hotel to pick up Lena. Her new flight out of Phoenix airport didn't leave until late tomorrow morning. But Dylan didn't want to take a chance on her staying in Tucson, so he found a new hotel outside the Phoenix airport.

Only Holmquist, Gonzalez and the Phoenix team knew about the change of plans. Dylan would inform the rest of the team when he arrived.

By now Chekowski should be with Joss. Everything should go smoothly. By acting quickly he was certain they'd fooled the Serpientes.

His phone buzzed. "Murphy."

Holmquist's voice echoed through the phone. "I'm here with Joss. Chekowski is the informer."

Several thoughts washed through Dylan's mind so fast, he couldn't put words together. When he finally got control, they came out in a jumble. "What? How? Is Joss safe?"

The officer's voice was soothing. "Take it easy. She managed to subdue him. A pretty good piece of officer work, if I say so myself."

Dylan didn't miss the pride in the older man's voice. He'd always known Holmquist felt an almost-paternal affection for Joss. Dylan had resented it before, thought it was getting in the way of his investigation. But now he was thankful the man cared so much.

"Joss heard Chekowski talking to someone from the gang. She thinks it might have been Vibora. Whoever it was, they know you are moving Lena Jones tonight."

Chekowski was the informer. It made sense. Dylan should have known…should have seen it. A major mistake. Now Joss *and* the transfer were both compromised. How much time did they have?

Dylan looked at the clock on his dash. "When did he talk to Vibora?"

"About twenty minutes ago. Just long enough for Joss to toss a pile of hay on his head and cuff him."

It almost sounded like Holmquist wanted to chuckle, but the circumstances were too dire. He didn't pause. "Even if the gang knows the plan, they haven't had much time to mobilize. Our best bet is to get Lena and her family out of there immediately."

"I agree. I'm minutes from her hotel. We'll put the

plan in action the second I get there. Hopefully we'll beat the gang."

"As soon as I hang up, I'll send reinforcements to your location."

"Thanks." Dylan clicked off the phone and hit the gas pedal. Speed was of the essence. He dialed Gonzalez. When his agent picked up the phone, Dylan was terse. "I'll be there in five. Have Lena and her family ready. We're moving immediately."

"Aren't we going to wait for the transport from Phoenix?"

"They're still en route and the Serpientes know our plans. Our only safety is in moving fast. Be ready. You'll drive them all the way to Phoenix."

"Maybe you should take them."

"I've got to get to Joss. She's already had to fend off Chekowski."

"Fend off? Did he attack her?"

"I'll fill you in when I get there. Just get Lena ready. Gonzalez…be on the alert. The Serpientes have beat us to the punch almost every time we've moved."

"We'll be ready."

He clicked off. Dylan threw his phone onto the passenger seat and sped through a yellow light. He was only blocks away, and he wasn't wasting time.

He pulled into the parking lot of the hotel. Lights blazed from the large paned windows of the lobby, and he eased his SUV as close to the door as he could, bumping over a cement border. He picked up his phone, pulled his gun and stepped out of the vehicle in one swift move.

He was parked less than seven feet from the entrance. A policeman and a hotel employee came running toward him at the same time. The employee reached him first.

"I'm sorry, sir. You simply can't park there."

He pulled out his badge. "Get all of your employees out of the lobby, to a safe location. We have word that gang members are on their way."

The young man looked around as if he wasn't sure what to do. The policeman running up behind him heard Dylan's command.

"Move, buddy. This place is about to light up."

Dylan gave the officer a look of thanks. He was older, close to Chekowski's age. Probably came up through the ranks with the traitor. Were they friends?

Dylan's jaw clenched. "How many of you are here?"

"Five, all stationed around the parking lot."

Dylan nodded. "No offense but I need you and your men to move away. Gather them up and head for the perimeter."

"You're calling us off?"

"Yeah. You can thank Chekowski. He told the gang about my witness."

The policeman sagged and shook his head. "That guy has always been trouble."

"Maybe. But I can't be sure I can trust any of you."

"I'll watch your back. If any of my officers turn, I'll take care of it."

Dylan gave the man a curt nod as he moved toward the elevator, calling the other agent.

"Gonzalez. I'm downstairs. Let's start the transfer."

"Got it."

Gonzalez knew the drill. The guards would clear the hallway upstairs. Then they'd lead Lena and her family out of the apartment and into the elevator. He waited, his gaze fixed on the lights above the elevator door.

He tensed as the numbers hit...three...two...one. The doors opened. Lena Jones was huddled in a corner with her arms around her four-year-old son. An older woman, obviously her mother, stood to one side and slightly behind her daughter.

Gonzalez was the first out. Dylan handed him his car keys. Gonzalez tossed the keys to his car.

"You'll need transportation to Joss." He didn't pause as he headed toward Dylan's parked vehicle. Lena Jones started out of the elevator, but Dylan held up his hand.

"Wait until he's in the car and situated."

The frightened woman picked up her child and grasped the arm of the older woman. Gonzalez started the ignition. Dylan motioned the women on. His men formed a barrier between the family and the hotel windows.

Just as they reached the car doors, Dylan heard a shout. He looked toward the parking lot and saw the group of policemen crouching down behind parked cars, facing the freeway on-ramp above them. Gunfire lit up the dark sky.

Dylan spun and shouted, "Move it!"

Lena had already stepped into the vehicle with her son. The older woman was having a hard time climbing up, so Dylan helped her into the car.

"Get on the floor." Both women obeyed him, and he ran to the rear of his vehicle.

The police fired more shots at the two cars that were parked on the freeway on-ramp above the hotel. The shooters had a perfect view of the front of the hotel and his men.

More gunfire lit up the night sky, and a bullet pinged off the roof of his SUV. The women inside screamed and his men ducked. They were pinned and couldn't cross the parking lot, to get to their own vehicles. If Dylan gave Gonzalez the go-ahead to drive off, he'd be on his own. The gang members could easily stop firing and follow him, leaving Dylan and his men in the lurch. He couldn't allow that to happen either.

Another barrage of gunshots. Bullets pinged around them.

The policeman—true to his word—along with his men, fired back, laying down a protective barrage. But they were all stuck like ducks in a shooting gallery. They couldn't stay here, but they couldn't move forward.

Just when Dylan thought he would have to pull Lena and her family back into the hotel, the blue lights of patrol cars flashed, headed toward the on-ramp and the shooters. The extra units Holmquist had sent had arrived.

The gang members stopped shooting. Dylan watched as the men scrambled into their cars and sped up the ramp, with the patrol units in close pursuit.

Dylan signaled his men to head to their vehicles. "Standard procedure," he called out as they hurried to their parked cars.

He looked at Gonzalez and his agent in the passenger seat. "Take no chances. Just get them safely to Phoenix."

He slammed the door and pounded the side. Gonzalez waved and pulled out. One vehicle screeched in front of him and another pulled in behind as they headed out of the parking lot.

Dylan heaved a sigh. Now to get Joss to safety.

After Holmquist hung up the phone, he roused Chekowski and herded him into the back of his car. Joss tried to reassure the anxious horses by petting them and talking to them in a calm voice. Surprisingly it helped her too. Then she fed them and gave them fresh water.

By the time Joss finished and headed to Holmquist's vehicle, darkness had fallen. Her supervisor gestured to where Chekowski leaned his head against the seat. "You clocked him pretty good."

Joss had no remorse. "Good. He deserves it. He got Henderson shot."

Holmquist hooked his thumbs in his belt. "You're sounding more and more like the agent I know so well."

"Am I?" Wrapping her arms around herself, she looked at the dark ranch house. It was an empty building, but it had come to mean more to her. A place of her own. Family. Someone beside her.

"I'm not sure I want to be that kind of agent anymore."

Her supervisor paused. "Joss, you are—"

She held up her hand. "Don't say it!" She smiled to soften her harsh tone. "Thank you for reminding me and caring so much. But maybe I'd like to be the kind of agent who has a home and a family."

He leveled a frowning gaze in her direction. "I suppose that home and family life would include one special agent named Murphy."

She shook her head and looked at the house. "You know that's not possible. Dylan Murphy is on a mission to save the world. Not just one foolish, somewhat-guilty border-patrol agent."

"Guilty?" He glanced sideways. "What do you have to feel guilty about?"

She shrugged. "Not reporting my brother when I began to suspect he was working for the gang. Not calling for backup when I saw those gang members leaving his apartment. I could have prevented everything else that happened after that."

"Maybe. We'll never know for sure. But we do know you were kidnapped, snatched right off the street. None of the rest of that matters."

"It matters to Dylan," she said in a low voice. "He might forgive that kind of mistake, but he won't forget and neither will I. It will always be between us."

Holmquist made a noise, then, flipping off his hat, beat it against his leg. "I warned him, told him not to use your feelings for him as a tool to solve his case."

Joss was so surprised by his anger toward Dylan, she was speechless. His affection for her brought tears to her eyes.

Reaching across the space, she touched his arm. "It's not like that, honestly. It isn't ambition or a sense of duty driving him." She paused and looked around.

"I didn't understand, didn't know how much he'd lost, until I came here. Then I saw how he'd been hurt and how deep it went."

She ducked her head and lowered her voice. "Now I understand. His guilt is heavier and stronger than mine ever will be. He can't forget it or defeat it." She met Holmquist's gaze and gave him a slight smile. "I can't either. It was silly of me to think I could."

The older man grasped her hand. "Joss…"

"It's all right." She gave him another half smile. "I may have lost that battle, but I've won one for myself." Her gaze roamed over the dark ranch house. "I've found what I really want. When this is all over, I'm going after it."

He squeezed her hand. "I hope that includes your life with us. You're—"

She laughed out loud. "I know. I'm a good agent."

Holmquist smiled. "Glad you finally got the message."

His radio squawked and he hurried to answer it. The border-patrol unit he'd contacted to pick up Chekowski was turning into the ranch's drive.

Joss caught his gaze and motioned to the house. "I'm going to get cleaned up."

By the time she'd showered and returned to the living room, Holmquist was stretched out on the couch, sound asleep after his long day.

Joss sat in one of the recliners and, in spite of her worry over Dylan, dozed. Finally the house phone rang. She jerked awake and ran to the kitchen, where sunshine flowed through the window. She grabbed the phone on the third ring.

"It's me." Dylan's voice eased over the receiver and she sighed in relief. Still, he sounded tired and frustrated. "I'm on my way to the station to make arrangements. Pack your bags, Joss. We'll be heading to Los Angeles when I return."

"Los Angeles? Why? What happened?"

He sounded tired and defeated. "Lena and her family are safe. I'll fill you in when I get there."

He hung up before she could say more.

Holmquist had followed her into the kitchen. She turned to him. "It's over. Lena is safe and Dylan's on his way to the station. I think he's putting me in protective custody in Los Angeles."

Her supervisor nodded. "A good move. You need to be far away while we get down to the business of arresting Vibora and Caulder. I'm going to check in with the station to see if those warrants have been processed." He lifted his cell and dialed as he walked to the front door.

Joss scrambled some eggs, and even managed to get a few bites down. Breakfast was an almost-silent affair. Holmquist looked tired and Joss's mind was on her move to LA. Although she knew it was for her own safety, she couldn't help but dread leaving the ranch... and Dylan. Once she did, everything between them would be over. The special glances. The shared moments and the unspoken bond. It would be severed as Dylan put on the armor of his mission.

Sadness dogged her movements as she packed her things. It only took fifteen minutes. Then she remembered the horses had been in their stalls since Dylan left. She hurried out. Holmquist followed her and helped her wrangle the bridles on, just before he got another call. The station's daily activities didn't slow down for this case, or for their supervisor's absence.

"My signal isn't strong here. I'll try inside." He headed into the house.

Joss led the horses from the barn and tied them on the fence for some fresh air and sunshine. This would be her last time with the magnificent animals. She grabbed the curry and began to brush.

The late-morning sun was gentle. A soft breeze tickled the tops of the cottonwoods and cooled the air. They rubbed together, creating a sound like rushing water. With one hand on Goldie's warm flank, and the soothing water sound above her, she closed her eyes and thanked God for this moment, for Dylan's safety, and that of Lena and her family. Most of her memory had returned. Some pieces were still missing, but she was thankful for what she had and for this moment of peace and beauty. She'd had so few recently.

The low thrum of an approaching engine broke through her prayer, and she opened her eyes. Thankfully she recognized the black government SUV. Dylan pulled up and eased out of the car, with his gaze fixed on her.

He looked exhausted, but a slow smile slipped over his lips. The look in his eyes was soft and possessive. He stood for a long moment, just looking at her until she stopped brushing and returned his stare. She could have stood in his gaze for the rest of her life.

But he slipped his baseball cap off and ran his fingers through his hair. The curls wrapped around his fingers and bounced back. She wanted to touch them, to feel those soft curls beneath her fingertips, to ease the exhaustion she saw in him. Instead she swallowed and turned to the horse.

Hanging his head, he ran a hand through his hair again. Did he realize that was the second time in less than five minutes?

He crossed over to her, patted Goldie and looked off into the distance. "You saved lives last night. Two cars full of gunmen sat on the freeway on-ramp above the hotel. They could have picked us off like they were target shooting. Thanks to you, we were prepared."

She smiled.

He met her gaze. "It isn't safe here any longer. We have to get you far away, and I can't have both of my star witnesses in the same location. I spent the rest of the night making arrangements for you in LA."

"I know."

Was his silence a sign of his disappointment? She wanted to ask. There was so much she wanted to say, but he looked toward the house. "Is Holmquist inside? I need to speak with him before he leaves."

Joss nodded and Dylan strode off. Reluctant to follow him, she continued brushing Goldie's coat. When she finished she went to the barn to muck out their stalls and brush up the hay she'd dumped on Chekowski. When she had it all stacked in a pile, she went outside. Goldie nickered a greeting. Smiling, she stroked his head and leaned her forehead against his.

Dylan and Holmquist exited the house. Her boss paused and stopped short of the horses. He fumbled with his hat. "Joss...be safe. I—"

Joss released the horse, hurried to his side and wrapped her arms around his waist for a big hug. "I'll be back soon. Don't worry."

Not able to find his voice, he nodded, slipped his hat on his head and headed for his car. Joss went to the horse to stroke his long muzzle. She couldn't watch as Holmquist headed down the dirt road.

"We'll have to leave soon, Joss. I just need a little break before I tackle the long road to California."

Joss's stomach sank to her feet, but she paused only for a moment before stroking Goldie. The horse's warm, smooth muscles and the reality of his big, strong body helped her stay grounded. She took a deep breath and ran her hand along the animal's back.

"I'll miss these guys." Her voice dropped. "They've helped me a lot. What'll happen to them?"

"I've called Hank. He's picking them up tomorrow."

"Can we...is there time for a short ride before I go?"

Dylan didn't answer for a long while. Finally she looked at him. He was exhausted. His shoulders sagged. A deep frown creased his brow. She could almost hear him waging a battle inside. But his hooded gaze softened when he looked at her.

"We shouldn't but I'd like that too...a lot. It'll have to be short though."

Joss didn't give him a chance to change his mind. She untied the horses and led them to the barn. In minutes they were saddled. Just before they climbed on, Dylan ran into the house for the cowboy hat Joss had worn the day before. She settled it on her head and they were off.

Instead of taking the river route, Dylan crossed the field and headed along a dirt road. He kicked Patches into a slight trot and glanced over to make sure Joss had managed the change of pace. She gave Goldie a nudge.

Dylan headed toward a distant peak that poked up out of the earth like a tall anthill. Joss smiled. Almost all of her memory had returned, but funny things jumped out in her mind, odd bits of info like those a child might discover.

They called the mountains in this area "islands in the sea." The mountain ahead of them was exactly like that—tall but surrounded by an ocean of flatland.

Dylan turned off the dirt trail and began to climb. Joss had to concentrate as Goldie picked her way around cacti, yuccas and saguaros. But there weren't too many of those plants. They didn't like the higher elevations and soon completely disappeared.

The horses had to work harder as they climbed. The sun beat down on them, but soon the cool breeze kicked up stronger. Clouds formed overhead. The late-afternoon monsoon was on its way, but Dylan didn't pause. He seemed determined to reach an overlook above them.

It was closer than it looked and came with a view for hundreds and hundreds of miles on three sides. One of the things Joss loved about the Southwest was the clear skies and the amazing visibility. Directly in front of them, Mexico rolled away in undulating plains. To their left, the San Pedro River Valley was dotted with square green patches of farms and ranches. On the right a natural desert was marked with the deep cutouts of streams and ravines that flowed toward the river.

Beside her, Patches shifted, and she looked at Dylan. He was watching her. The possessive look in his gaze made her heart skip a beat. If only…

Joss turned away. There could never be an "if only" for her and Dylan. His one and only love was his work. No matter how much she…or he…might wish it, Dylan had no room in his life for the things Joss had come to realize she needed…trust, companionship and a safe, happy place to call home. Dylan could never provide those things for her. She understood now, and she was never going down that path of wishful thinking again.

The cell phone attached to his belt buzzed three times in quick succession. He lifted it and glanced at the readout. "I guess we were behind the mountain. I wasn't getting reception. Holmquist has been trying to reach me."

He punched the button. Because of the silence on the lookout, the voice on the phone came to Joss loud and clear.

"Murphy, this is Holmquist. I got a call from the station. The guys transporting Chekowski were fired on. One officer was wounded. But Chekowski was the target. He was dead on the scene." There was a pause. "It was a drive-by shooting, and the vehicle was a gray Toyota. We alerted the local police and state troopers to be on the lookout. The truck was spotted heading onto I-10. The troopers set up a watch along the interstate. If the truck heads your way, I'll keep you posted."

Dylan looked up. Joss's expression must have shown

her concern, because he said, "They couldn't be on us that quickly. Chekowski told them you weren't here. They have to be headed someplace else."

He punched the message. "Murphy. Bad news. The truck and three other vehicles pulled off the interstate, onto Highway 91. They're headed your way. Get out of there."

Dylan didn't look at her. He selected the next message. "Answer me, Murphy. I need to know where you are. We're on our way, but Vibora and Caulder have a jump on us. Get out of there!"

Dylan slid the phone onto his belt. Without turning to her, he pulled on Patches' reins. "We're going to make fast time. Keep up the pace as best as you can."

They spun the horses around and looked back the way they'd come. Far off in the distance a rooster tail of dust flew high in the air. The gray Toyota truck and three SUVs were on a dirt road headed their way.

Dylan watched the cavalcade coming fast and couldn't believe his eyes. How had the gang figured out Chekowski's mistake so soon? Now they were trapped. No way could they make it to the ranch. Vibora and his men were between them and safety.

Stupid. Stupid. Stupid. He'd wanted one last ride. He'd let down his guard and allowed himself this perfect moment, and now Joss's life was in danger. How could he be so foolish?

He looked to the mountaintop. "They must have seen us climbing the hill from the ranch. We can't go back there. We have to go up. It's only a thousand more feet.

Fatal Memories

The horses can make it. On the other side of that peak is Sierra Vista and the local police. Vibora's vehicles can't climb up there. Let's go."

Clicking Patches into motion, he pulled out his phone and dialed Holmquist. Reception was spotty, but the man's message machine picked up. Dylan gave him their location and where they were headed, but he had no idea if it went through or stalled behind the mountain—and they didn't have time to wait for an answer. They needed to put as much distance between themselves and the gang as possible.

He cut across through the rough terrain and looked back. Joss was managing to keep up. She was a natural, but they'd already been in the saddle too long. Sooner or later she'd feel the strain and they'd have to slow down. They needed to go high and far—fast.

They climbed steadily. The shrub and piñon trees gave way to taller species—Arizona white oak, sycamores and an occasional pine. Finally they reached the covering of a forest of white oak. Dylan breathed a sigh of relief. At least now Vibora and his crowd couldn't see them on the mountainside and spot their location. They were shielded by the trees.

The afternoon clouds had gathered into a dark cluster overhead. Rain wouldn't be far behind and it would fall in a deluge. They needed to find temporary shelter, something that would protect the horses and give them a rest, because as soon as the storm cleared, they would be riding again.

He searched the area. Nothing. No place to hide or shield them.

Thunder cracked right over their heads and Goldie jumped, skittering to the side. Joss almost lost her seat. He kicked Patches ahead to catch her. At the last minute she managed to right herself, but lightning crackled and Goldie skittered again. He slowed his pace and stayed right beside Joss as lightning and thunder boomed around them, keeping the horses skittish and jumpy.

I have to find shelter. We can't keep this up.

The clouds opened and rain poured on them. In seconds, Joss was soaked. Her T-shirt clung to her body, and her ponytail sagged down her back. Dylan's cowboy hat gave her some protection, but soon water poured off the brims of both their hats, blinding them. The rain lightened somewhat, but the wind whipped up, slanting the rain sideways so that it pounded them like little splinters.

The horses were almost ready to bolt. "Get off, Joss," he shouted. "Walk Goldie and talk to him. He's afraid."

Not even trying to answer, she slid off the animal. Grasping the reins, she comforted the horse and stroked his muzzle. Dylan followed her actions and strode on, barely able to see through the growing gloom of the storm-darkened skies.

Finally he found a massive outcropping of boulders that was surrounded by trees. It didn't provide an overhang for them to shelter beneath, but it did have a leeward side…away from the pelting rain. He motioned to Joss and hurried forward. As soon as he rounded the boulder, the piercing rain was broken. He breathed a sigh and turned Patches so the horse stood sideways, pressed against the rear of the shelter. Joss did the same and soon they were lined up, back-to-back, facing their horses, comforting them and speaking in low tones.

The rain pounded on and on. Dylan glanced over his shoulder to check on Joss, but that's all the attention he could give her. She had a good handle on the horse, but she was sagging, tired and worn-out. He called himself another choice name.

This high on the mountain, maybe he could get service on his cell phone. With one hand he flipped out his phone and searched for a signal. Nothing. Patches neighed and sidled again, so he slid the phone into his belt and barely managed to get a hold of the horse.

Aided by the cloudy sky, the temperature dropped. The rain eased to a drizzle. The horses calmed and Dylan was able to give Joss more attention. Shivering, she leaned against Goldie, barely able to stand, weary from riding and wrangling the spooked horse. She needed to rest before they started riding again. She wouldn't make it without a break. He tied Patches to a nearby tree, then went for Goldie. Taking the reins from Joss's cold fingers he pushed her toward the rock. "Sit. Rest."

She put her arms around herself and slid to the ground, leaning against the boulder.

As soon as Goldie was tied off, he hurried back. Sitting beside Joss, he wrapped his arm around her and held her close. At first she resisted, but her body was cold and he was warmer. After a moment she eased into him. He pressed his lips to the top of her head. She buried her face in his neck.

"Bad things happen after a storm. My father was

killed after a storm like this." Her teeth chattered around the words.

He rubbed his hands up and down her back, chafing them for heat. "I'm glad you're remembering things, but this has nothing to do with a storm. It's my fault. I never should have agreed to the ride. I just thought I could steal a few more minutes with you."

She looked up, her eyes wide and full of want. "I'd give you all my minutes if you'd let me."

Her lips were almost blue and so close, he couldn't resist. He dipped his head and kissed her cold, cold mouth. She tasted cool and sweet like the rain, and her body felt soft in his arms.

It was all he could do to break the kiss and turn his gaze away. "Believe me, you don't want that, Joss. It would only mean more trouble for you. Look what happened. I let my guard down and once again the person I care about most in the world is in danger. If that's not God telling me to stay focused, I don't know what is."

Joss shook her head and tried to speak, but a violent shiver shook her. He tightened his arms around her, trying to warm her.

He wanted to apologize, to say he was sorry again. But saying sorry wouldn't get them over the mountain. What was needed now was his legendary focus. His determination. He needed to get her to safety. So he said nothing.

Into the silence came the sound of all-terrain vehicles. The gang must have transported them in the backs of their trucks. The whine of the quads' winding engines echoed through the forest. Joss turned to him, her eyes wide and frightened.

"Let's go." He lurched to his feet and pulled her up. They ran to the horses and untied them. He was in his seat like a flash, and watched as Joss clambered more slowly into her saddle. Just as she settled into it, he slapped Goldie on the flank and the animal jolted up the mountainside. Dylan kicked Patches into motion and took the lead. He grabbed Goldie's reins. "Hang on!"

Pulling the horse forward, he kicked Patches again. They lunged up the steep bank, dodging trees, weaving in and out of shrubs. The going was tough where rain-slicked leaves made the horses' hooves slip. They were forced to slow until they reached clear ground. Then Dylan kicked them for speed. And always the whine of the ATVs followed, growing closer and closer. As best as he could tell there were four vehicles.

Climbing at such a breakneck speed was hard on the animals. Their sides heaved with effort. Joss barely clung to the saddle horn as they bounced and jostled. He looked up. If they could make it to the peak… Not far on the other side was a ranger station and cabins. They could find help if they could reach the top.

A shot rang out and the bullet hit a tree to their left. Joss screamed. Goldie reared slightly. Dylan jerked on the reins, pulling to the right just before another shot rang out. This time the bullet went far and wide. Where did it land? He didn't hear or see it. He let the horses go for a few more paces, and then he turned them to the right. He had to zigzag. Keep them changing direction so the shooter or shooters couldn't zero in on them.

The next shot hit a tree on their right. Too close. The shooter had figured out their pattern and was anticipating their direction.

Go straight. Break the pattern again.

He kicked Patches and the sturdy horse bolted right through a six-foot-high brush…and straight out of the concealing forest. No trees to shelter them to the right or left, just a patch of rock and boulders leading to the peak. Even in the dusk of the cloud-filled sky, the gang could spot Joss's white T-shirt. She would be an easy target on top of the horse.

Dylan pointed Patches toward the nearest pile of rocks, then pulled both horses to an abrupt halt. After sliding off, he turned Patches loose and slapped him on the rump. The animal raced away. Reaching up, he pulled Joss out of the saddle and pushed her toward the rocks. Then he set Goldie free. The horse galloped away as a bullet pinged off a rock beside Dylan.

If he could hold them off until darkness fell…

He worked his way to the highest point of the cluster of boulders. He slipped off his dark shirt and gave it to Joss to cover her white T-shirt, ignoring the fact that his white T-shirt, which he had on under his dark shirt, now made him an easy target.

"Run for that peak." He pointed out where he wanted her to go. "I'll hold them off. You should be able to see the ranger station. Head for that."

"No. I won't leave you."

He grasped both of her arms. "You have to. Have you forgotten your brother and Maria? If Vibora gets his hands on you, he will use you to drive your brother out of hiding and he won't make it easy on you or Jason."

She shook her head. "I won't leave you behind."

"We're here because of me. Give me the chance to make it right."

She shook her head again. He pushed her away. "Go before it's too late for both of us."

She took a few steps, but then halted.

"Go, Joss, now! I'll never forgive myself if you die."

Sobbing, she spun and ran up the hill. Dylan prayed the storm would protect her. Then he turned to face a line of bushes below him. From the sound of it, the ATVs were almost there. Gripping his wrist, he slowed his breathing and prepared to take aim.

An ATV broke through the brush. Not far behind was another. Dylan aimed at the lead rider and fired. The man cried out and fell off the quad. The machine shot off into the forest, riderless, with the engine still thrumming.

The driver behind screeched his vehicle to a halt, kicking up dirt and dust. The second man on the back jumped off. He grabbed the man on the ground and dragged him to the clump of bushes while the driver flipped the vehicle around and sped back the way he'd come. Dylan fired at him but missed.

Make those count. You don't have enough bullets for wild shots.

The engines died and there was a momentary silence.

Good. They hadn't realized he was armed until he had fired. His shot sent a clear warning and slowed their pace. Now they were trying to figure out what to do. That would give Joss more time to reach the peak.

The engines started up again. Dylan tensed. *Why now? What did they see that spurred them into action so quickly?*

Turning to look behind him, he spotted Joss on the precipice of the peak, silhouetted against the gray sky.

He spun back. The ATVs shot out of the bushes, rushing his location. He fired a shot and hit one man. He didn't fall off his quad but he cried out. Dylan missed another. A shot pinged the rock next to him and he had to duck, but just for a moment. He popped out again. Two of the vehicles were closer.

While he fired at the two vehicles, the third ATV shot around the other side of the cluster of boulders, headed for the top. Dylan spun and fired at the two men on the machine but missed. The vehicle wove in and out of trees, and he couldn't get a clear shot.

He ran to the end of the boulders as the engine slowed. He couldn't see Joss, but he heard a scream echo over the mountainside. The engine revved again and the sound traveled farther and farther away.

They got her! The men on the quad got her. Dylan sagged against the rock. The other ATVs shot by him, heading for the top. Now that they had Joss, they didn't waste time or bullets on him. They left Dylan alone… stranded on the mountain.

He'd failed. He pounded his fist against the rock and cried out. His anguished scream was lost in the ascending motors of the ATVs.

Why? Why God? Why do You let me fail when it means the most to me?

Because you believe you deserve it.

Joss's words echoed in his mind. She was right. It wasn't God punishing him, denying him happiness and a life outside of his work. God had given him Joss. A beautiful gift. A companion in his life, a bright memory amongst all the dark ones. But Dylan was too stubborn, too stuck on his own guilt to recognize what he'd been given.

All the time Joss had been dealing with her guilt, the Lord was talking to Dylan too, trying to show him how to let go of his own blame. Instead he'd shoved her guilt back at her, accused her of wrongdoing and made everything worse.

The words of Joss's scripture came to him. *Persecuted, but not forsaken; cast down, but not destroyed.*

How he wished he'd listened. But now it was too late. He'd lost his chance. Vibora had Joss, and he would make her pay…and there was no way Dylan could stop it.

The image of Beth in her coffin popped into his mind; only this time, Joss lay inside. Dylan cried out and dropped to his knees. His body sagged. His weapon tumbled to the ground, and tears mixed with the rain on his cheeks.

Joss was squeezed between the two men on the quad. The man behind her had a knife pressed against her throat, and every movement, every bump of the machine caused the sharp, flat blade to pierce her skin. She was terrified, shaking so much that she bumped against the edge on her own. Blood dripped from her neck onto Dylan's shirt as they descended the other side of the mountain.

It didn't make sense. Where were they taking her? They had tried to kill her twice. Now they wanted her alive. What had changed?

Where was Dylan? Had he been shot? Was he lying somewhere on the hill? She closed her eyes as trembling took over her body. The man behind her laughed, a cruel, vicious chuckle that made tears run down her cheeks.

There would be no help there. She couldn't expect an ounce of compassion from the gang members. She was on her own.

The man in front had headphones over his head with an attached microphone. He spoke into the thin microphone, giving someone their location and telling them where to meet them. She guessed the vehicles she and Dylan had seen in the distance would be waiting for them at the base of the mountain.

This side of the peak had much more vegetation. The quad wove in and out of trees and shrubs. It took longer to descend. Ahead she could see a cluster of buildings. The ranger station.

The cloudy sky decreased visibility, but there was some daylight. Maybe someone would see them. Hope rippled over her skin like a shiver.

But the driver turned away, skirting far from the buildings. The man behind her pulled her against him and pressed the flat, sharp blade to her throat.

"Yell for help, *chica*. Make me happy."

Joss froze. They passed the gathering of buildings and Joss didn't move, didn't even breathe. The man's sinister chuckle echoed in her ear before he lowered the knife.

Finally they reached a paved road at the base of the hill, where a tan SUV waited. The men on the quad pulled up. Several others jumped out of the vehicle, including the man with the shaved head and snake tattoo on his neck, the one Dylan called Snake Man. None too gently he bound Joss's hands with plastic ties, gagged her and bundled her into the back of the SUV.

The men climbed into the front seat and sped away. Joss silently shivered and trembled. Had she survived just so she would be back where she'd started? Had Dylan sacrificed...?

No. She wouldn't go there. He couldn't be dead. God wouldn't let it happen. They had come too far to let it end this way. Dylan was alive and he was coming for her.

She needed to stay strong, to fight her captors every step of the way. Determination filled her. Slowly but surely she controlled her trembling. She needed to see where they were going. She wanted to remember where they were taking her. Never again did she want to have the helpless, hopeless feeling of not knowing.

With her hands tied behind her, she couldn't use them to lift herself, so she twisted until her feet were against one side and her back against the other. Then she wedged herself up so she could look out the window.

They'd driven into the city of Sierra Vista. The streets were full of cars and people. The SUV stopped at a stoplight. In the lane beside them a man sat in his car, with the windows rolled down. If she could get his attention… She began to make muffled noises and kick the window. If he would just look up and see the gag in her mouth, he might report it to the police!

"Shut her up!" the man in the front seat yelled, and Snake Man bent over the seat and pushed her down, pressing her face into the carpet so hard, she could barely breathe. After a moment she grew light-headed and stopped struggling. The man released her. She lay very still, sucking in air.

They drove for a long while. The sounds of the city faded. They traveled over hills and dips. She thought they might be driving through the hilly country of Patagonia. That meant they were headed to Nogales. Were they taking her someplace across the border to be shot and left in the vast deserts, where she would never be found? Her heart pounded so hard, she felt nauseous. If she threw up now, with the gag in her mouth, she could very well choke to death. Closing her eyes, she slowed her breathing.

The nausea abated. Her heart stopped racing. She rested, gathering her strength for what came next.

They pulled off to the side of the road. The men stepped out. She wedged herself up to see. They milled around, talking and…waiting. For what?

It seemed like hours had passed. Joss needed a drink. Her hands were numb, her senses dulled, and still they waited. Finally a car pulled up and stopped. A man came to the back and opened the hatch.

They're going to kill me and dump me in the woods.

Not without a fight!

Gathering her energy after hours of immobility, she kicked at the man at the hatch until Snake Man climbed into the back seat and placed a gun against her temple.

"Be still, little girl, or my friend will be cleaning up a mess in his car." His voice was low and raspy, like sandpaper. Just the sound of it, let alone the words, stopped her cold.

The man at the back dragged her across the carpet of the hatch and pulled her out. Another car had pulled up behind them. The car's headlights nearly blinded her. She ducked her head and wobbled as her captor stood her on her feet, which were numb. The passenger-side door opened. A man climbed out. Short. Wiry. He walked toward her with a swagger that set alarm bells ringing in her head.

She knew that walk. Memories flooded into her mind...of Vibora leaning over her, screaming, *Where did your traitor brother take my sister?*

She kept her eyes lowered and ducked away from the headlights.

Vibora dipped his head low, trying to see her eyes. When she didn't look up, he grasped her chin in a vicious grip and forced it up. She refused to show him fear, so she schooled her features.

He studied her for a long while. "They say you do not remember me."

Something sank inside of her. She knew this man's reputation, knew his viciousness made an imprint everywhere he went. No way would she give in, show him the fear he wanted to see. He released her chin and leaned in close. "Where is your brother? Where did he hide my sisters and mother?"

She shook her head. Vibora motioned the man holding her arms to remove the gag.

The sudden release of the tight binding brought tears to her eyes. She tried to lick her lips, but they were so dry, the motion hurt.

Vibora was in her face again. Fury radiated from him, and his hot breath fell against her skin like burning acid. She flinched and turned her head.

"Where are they?"

"I don't know."

He grasped her chin and forced her to look at him again. "Lie to me and I will make you pay."

For the first time she met his gaze, but she was careful to erase any fear or anger from her features. She stared at him, wide-eyed.

"I...don't...know. I don't even remember my brother," she lied. Was she too scared to make the lie convincing?

His dark gaze glared into hers, pinning her, holding her prisoner not only with his fingers but with those black eyes. Apparently she was successful. He released her.

"So it's true you don't know who I am." He nodded once and then stepped behind her. His fingers grazed her neck as he slid her ponytail away and leaned in. His lips were so close to her ear that his whispered words made a shiver trip up her spine.

"Soon you will know exactly who I am. I will make you remember, and you will never forget me...for as long as you live."

She caught her breath but had no time to respond. The

man with the tattooed snake writhing on his neck picked her up and threw her bodily into the back, then slammed the hatch. The SUV sped off into the black night.

NINE

The storm finally cleared. But still the cloud cover brought darkness to this side of the mountain. Dylan had combed the area, looking for Patches and Goldie. He could travel faster with them, but he'd already wasted precious time searching. He couldn't afford to look for much longer.

He slipped on a rock hidden by wet leaves and went down hard on one knee for the second time. The pain held him still for a moment and he sagged. Tired and thirsty, he took a deep breath.

Lord, help me. Don't let Joss suffer for my mistakes. Help me.

In the silence he heard another sound. ATVs. More than one, coming up the hill from all directions. He gritted his teeth. The gang had returned to finish him off.

He checked his weapon. Only a few bullets left. Looking around, he spotted another clump of boulders. If he could hide there, maybe he could get close enough to unseat one of the riders and take the quad. He might not get far. They'd probably shoot him or overtake him, but he had to try. Had to get to Joss.

After climbing stiffly to his feet, he ducked behind some boulders. He found a deep crevice to hide in.

The ATVs came closer. Dylan tensed, praying he had enough cover. He cocked his gun. One of the machines sounded close, very close. He peeked out enough to see it was not more than twenty feet away. As he retreated, something clicked in his vision.

He'd seen the green-and-yellow patches of the border-patrol uniform. Did the ATVs belong to officers who were looking for him? Was it possible? Clicking the lock on his gun in place, he decided to take a chance.

Holding his hands high above his head, he stepped out from his hiding place. The ATV's headlights bounced over him. The engine decelerated, making it easy to hear the crackle of a radio and a woman's voice.

"I've found them. Agent Murphy is alive!"

"Jenny?"

"Yes, it's me." She stepped off the ATV and walked into the glare of the headlights. "Departments came out of the woodwork when word went out that the gang was headed your way. Good thing too. We would never have found you if a ranger hadn't reported suspicious activity on the mountain."

More headlights bounced through the forest as other vehicles headed their way. As the officers gathered around him, he realized it was a search party of border-patrol officers, as well as park rangers and local police, but none of his DEA agents. Where were they?

"They got Joss, Jenny. Vibora's men took her."

Another man drove up and dismounted. "Good to see you, Murphy."

Dylan shook his outstretched hand. "Trust me, you'll never know how relieved I am to see you. But they have Officer Walker. I've got to get on their trail before it grows cold." He looked around. "Where's Holmquist?"

Jenny paused. "We might know where they're taking her. Holmquist and some of your unit are gearing up for a raid on the gang's safe house now. That's why he's not here."

"What? They know where they are taking Joss?"

"An informant called it in and gave us the exact location."

"An informant? Who is that brave soul?"

"Jason Walker."

"Joss's brother?" He repeated the words as if he'd never heard them before. "That's why they snatched her instead of just shooting us both and leaving us on the mountain. They know Walker is back. They're going to use her to force him into the open. Thanks to him we're a step ahead of them!"

Joss's scripture came to him.

Persecuted, but not forsaken; cast down, but not destroyed.

Not forsaken. God had not abandoned him, even though he deserved it. The good Lord was giving him a second chance through, of all people, the man who had left Joss to face Vibora alone.

If this second chance wasn't proof of God's mercy, Dylan didn't know what was.

Mindless of the revelation rocking Dylan's brain,

Jenny continued speaking. He struggled to focus on her words.

"Jason's been out of touch. He destroyed all of their phones and computers. Used cash to travel and hid Maria and her family in Colorado. Then he tried to contact Joss. When he couldn't reach her, he headed back. As soon as he got into town, he called us."

"Why did he wait until he got into town to call?"

The woman shrugged. "We think he has a plan. Holmquist believes he's headed to the hideout. Walker said something about none of them being safe until Vibora is dead. Holmquist thinks Walker is going to try to take matters into his own hands."

"Your boss is right. I understand Jason completely. He feels the need to atone for his mistake, and so do I."

A puzzled frown filtered over Jenny's features, but she didn't waste time with questions. "We are mobilizing quickly."

"Where is this house?"

"In Nogales."

"How fast can you get me there?"

Jenny turned to a park ranger, who had shut off his engine and joined them.

"The fastest way is over the mountaintop," the man said. "I'll contact my men and they'll have a car waiting for you at the station."

Dylan nodded. "Thank you. I have two horses running loose here, in the forest. Can you track them down and take care of them for me?"

"We'll find them."

Dylan tipped his head again, then slid onto the ATV.

Determination filled him. He wasn't wasting a minute of this second chance.

"Let's go." Jenny gunned the engine and they sped out, kicking gravel up behind them.

Joss twisted and pulled on the zip ties around her wrist. Pain shot through her arms, with the warm wash of blood. Sighing, she eased her head onto the floor. Fighting was getting her nowhere. She needed to conserve strength for when they reached wherever they were taking her. That's when the real fight would begin. She needed to be alert, strong and ready.

Closing her eyes, she willed her tight shoulders to relax. She worked her jaw back and forth, forcing herself to release the taut tension. Then she closed her eyes and concentrated on her next steps.

City lights appeared. The vehicle stopped at a stoplight. Joss raised herself just enough to peek out the window. The Nogales Border Patrol Station was less than one hundred yards away. She didn't make the mistake of trying to get attention again. She eased down and waited.

They must have a safe house someplace in the city of Nogales, right near the border. Maybe once they arrived she could get free, cause a ruckus and catch the authorities' attention some other way. But the SUV drove a long way from the station, and her hopes sank. Nogales wasn't a large town. The safe house must be on the outskirts, far from any help.

The car stopped. The hatch opened, and Snake Man pulled her out again. He stood her on wobbly legs, and she stared at the house in front of them. The dirt yard looked like something between a used car lot and a wrecking yard. From beat-up and rusted clunkers to luxury sedans, vehicles faced every which direction. Lights blazed from all of the windows, without the slightest hint of movement behind them. Was anyone inside?

"Where's Antonio?"

"He must be in the hole. Go inside and check on him."

The hole? An underground storage or another tunnel? If they took her through to the other side of the border, her chances of getting free would decrease.

Other cars pulled up behind them. The large man shoved her forward. She tripped on the steps of the porch and he shoved her upright. Inside, she ducked her head from the bright lights. Someone set a chair in the middle of the room, and her guard pushed her onto it. At least seven gang members milled about inside the house. Who knew how many were pulling up in the cars outside?

Through the large front window, she could see a wiry form crossing the porch. Her stomach clenched. Vibora. He stalked into the room and headed straight for her. The wavering light made the tattoos of coiling serpents covering both his arms appear like they were slithering up and down.

"I'll give you one more chance. Where is your brother?"

Fear pooled in her belly like cold steel. "I don't know."

He pulled out a knife and placed the sharp blade

against her cheek. "Maybe if I cut your pretty face, you'll remember."

"I can't tell you what I don't know."

Even if she had known Jason's location, no way would she reveal it to this monster. She would give her life to protect her brother and Maria Martinez. Defiance filled her.

She glared at the man in front of her. "Besides, you're going to kill me anyway."

He stepped back and clicked the knife into itself. "Too bad for you. Maybe if you knew, I might make your death a little easier. Now I'll make sure it's slow and painful. Lots of pain. Lots of blood." He ran his finger down her arm on a slow path, clearly savoring the feel of her skin. "Then when you're dead, I will post pictures of your beautiful body, cut and bleeding, all over the internet, for your big brother to see what he has done to you. He'll pay for taking my sisters from me."

She might have resisted him, might have held out against his threats and the pain. But to think of Jason seeing her that way, feeling responsible...her eyes stung and then burned, and tears began to trickle.

"So, you remember your brother...the traitor?" He leaned in close again; his breath was so full of hot viciousness, she cringed and turned her head away. He grasped her chin and forced her to look. Brandishing the knife inches from her eyes, he clicked it open again. "He will pay for taking my family. I'll cut you. Then I'll make him watch while I cut my treacherous sister. My mother and my sister will never betray me again."

The thought of his mother watching her daughter

die punctured Joss's heart. And Vibora's little sister…
she was only ten. The idea of that child watching such
a horrific act overcame Joss. A sob broke through her
iron control and Vibora smiled. He didn't just use fear
to gain control and power over his drug kingdom. He
enjoyed the torture, thrilled at the aspect of people suffering. The man was out of his mind. Crazy enough to
frighten and control the brutal men surrounding him.

How would she get through what he had planned for
her? A terrified plea went through her.

Please, Lord.

The silent prayer comforted her. She knew she had
not been abandoned. Come what may, He would be
with her.

*You will be with me. You will give me strength. I
know it.*

She closed her eyes. Warmth swept through, calming
her trembling fingers. Vibora laid the knife against her
cheek again, placed its sharp edge close to her eye. Just
a little more pressure and he would have his first cut.

Suddenly one of the guards behind them made a
sound. "What the…?"

Vibora lowered the knife and walked around in front
of her. His body blocked her view. She strained her neck
to see around him as the guard lowered his gun and
backed from the doorway.

Her brother stepped into the room.

"Jason." His name slipped from her lips in a whisper.

His bloodshot eyes and mussed hair bore witness to
trials of his own. He wore beige cargo pants and a gray

T-shirt…and duct-taped over the shirt were small, gray packets of explosives.

"Cut her once, Vibora, and we all die."

Joss moaned, unprepared for the wave of relief brought on by the sound of her beloved brother's voice. Vibora cursed and moved toward him.

Jason held up his hand. "Don't come any closer." He gestured to his arm. "The detonator is beneath my arm. If it lowers even a quarter of an inch, these packets will ignite. This is all that's left of your supply, and you know there's enough here to make sure everyone in this house dies."

Vibora halted. His body stiffened, then he slowly shook his head. "You won't kill your little sister, the one you spoke about so often with such pride."

Jason's fist clenched. "I'll do whatever it takes to end your insane rampage of fear and murder."

Vibora loosened his grip on the knife in his hand. Then he shook his head and gestured over his shoulder to Joss. "Does she know about you? Does she know you broke the law, built our tunnels and betrayed her?"

Jason's jaw tightened and his fist clenched, but he never took his eyes off Vibora. "She knows I'll do anything to protect the ones I love. Anything. I broke the law for Maria and I'll die to keep her safe from you. I'll never let you get close to her again."

"You!" Vibora lunged at him.

Jason shouted, "Lucan! Stop him! You know I mean what I say."

Caulder grabbed Vibora's shoulder. "He'll do it.

Don't let your anger get us killed. Listen to what he has to say."

When Vibora didn't loosen his stance, Caulder shook his shoulder. "Live for another day."

Vibora jerked his shoulder loose from the other man's grip. A taut silence followed while he shifted his body, as if trying to gain control. All the while Vibora's piercing dark gaze, the one that had held Joss prisoner before, never moved off Jason.

At last Vibora spat, "What do you want?"

Jason pointed to Joss. "My sister and I are going to walk out of here. It's as simple as that. You let us go and you live. If not, we all die."

Vibora shook his head, but Caulder stepped closer. "Let him go." He dropped his voice. "We found him once. We'll find him again."

Those words gave Vibora pause and sent a sinking feeling through Joss because they were true. She and Jason might walk out of here now, but they would never be free. They would always be living in the shadows, wondering when Vibora would find them. Until he was dead or behind bars, they'd never be safe.

Vibora nodded slowly. "All right. You go free."

Joss could almost hear him thinking the words *this time*.

Jason pointed to Joss. "Cut her loose."

Caulder sliced the zip ties around her wrists with Vibora's knife. Blood rushed into her hands, crippling them with a burning pain. She gripped them, shaking and squeezing as Jason gestured Vibora and Caulder away from her.

"Don't forget. A quarter-of-an-inch drop in my arm sets these off."

Vibora's jaw clenched in frustration, but he backed away.

Jason hurried to her side and helped her stand on legs that trembled. She gripped his arm. He clasped her hand but kept her well away from the explosives strapped to his chest. He walked backward to the door, pushing Joss ahead of him, never turning from the men in the room and the guns trained on them. Jason opened the front door and paused. Reaching his free hand into his pocket, he pulled out a set of keys.

"There's a gray car parked in front of a house down the road. Go get it. I can't go too far away where the explosives can't reach them." He nudged his chin to the men in the room. "As soon as you get the car, drive up here and pick me up. We'll leave together."

And then they'll start shooting at us! We'll never get away fast enough! They'll blast us to pieces before we're out of this driveway.

Joss started to protest. Surely there was another way. But she couldn't think, couldn't see a way clear. They were trapped and this was their only chance at escape. She took the keys and gripped Jason's hand. He squeezed hers but never looked away from their captors. Tears filled her eyes as she ran into the dark night.

Armed with more bullets, Dylan shimmied up the side of a hill, almost on all fours. He lay next to Holmquist, who glanced over.

"Good to see you alive."

"Good to be alive." Joss's supervisor asked no questions about why Dylan had been so far out of cell-phone reach and did not mention the major blunder of letting the gang capture Joss. For that Dylan was grateful. An accounting of his mistakes would have to happen, but this was not the time. Now he had to concentrate on getting Joss to safety.

Three hills surrounded a small clearing below. The house sat to the back of the property. Cars were parked out front. To Dylan's left, lights blazed from every window in a second house.

Holmquist gestured to the structure. "We evacuated that place about an hour ago. The local police came in unmarked cars, established a perimeter around the house and evacuated the family. They'll be at the police station until this is over. We wanted to keep them under watch in case they have connections to the gang."

"Do they?"

"Nothing so far. In fact the father seems to be happy we're finally doing something about his neighbors."

"Joss is here?"

"She arrived about ten minutes ago." He pointed to a distant hill. "A man with binoculars has a decent view of her through a window. So far they're holding her... waiting for Vibora. He arrived about five minutes ago."

"What about Walker?"

"No sign of him. But the police have been here long enough to send in the license plates of every vehicle out front. They're all registered to Tucson citizens, except for that gray sedan in front of the house next to us. It's registered to a rental company at the airport."

"So, Walker's here."

"We think he's inside, but we haven't been able to see him…or what's going on. There's a guard at the back and one out front."

As he spoke the front door opened. Light fell from the portal and landed like a golden square on the dark yard in front of the house. Joss and Jason Walker appeared in the doorway. Dylan tensed.

She's alive.

One of the agents made a noise. "Looks like explosives strapped to Walker's chest."

Holmquist lifted the binoculars. "He's got the detonator beneath his arm. He's holding the gang off, keeping them inside."

The other agent shook his head. "How do they hope to get away?"

Joss grabbed something from her brother's hand and darted across the yard.

"She's going for her brother's car."

"Is she abandoning him?" the agent asked.

"Not Joss…she'd never do that." Dylan's tone was firm.

Holmquist let the binoculars drop. "As soon as they get clear of the house, the gang will use all of their firepower and blow them sky-high. They won't stand a chance."

Determination settled in Dylan. "They need their own firepower." He started to shimmy down. "As soon as I start firing, signal your men to open up on the house. And, Holmquist, tell them that no matter what happens to the Walkers and me, they are to keep firing. We can't let any of that gang free to hurt more people."

Dylan sidled down the hill. When he reached the base, he darted across the street and hid behind the vehicle. He could hear Joss's running feet and heavy breathing. As soon as she opened the car door, he stepped out.

"Hey, hotshot."

She jumped and almost screamed, but Dylan was prepared. He leaped forward and placed his fingers against her lips. "It's me. It's all right."

He didn't care if they didn't have a future or that he didn't deserve her love. He just wanted to touch her, to reassure himself that she was still alive. Cupping her cheeks with both hands, he kissed her, all the while thanking God that he'd found her alive.

"I thought you were dead," she whispered. "I thought they killed you on the mountain."

He shook his head. "You were the goal. As soon as they had you, they left me where I was. Didn't even bother to waste more ammunition on me."

She stepped back. "How did you get here? What's going on?"

"Jason called in the location. This place is surrounded with police, border-patrol and DEA agents. We're going to get both of you out of here."

She leaned into his hands, which were still cupped to her face. "Thank you. Thank you."

Dylan ducked his head to catch her gaze. "Let's go get Jason. You drive. I'll ride low in the passenger seat, next to you, so they won't see me. As soon as you get in the car, roll down my window so all I have to do is pop up and start firing…and I'll need to shoot straight. No matter what he said, Vibora doesn't plan to let you get away. Pull up on the door so that Jason has to get in the back seat. I'll make sure he's situated. You concentrate on driving. When I give you the signal, hit the gas and get us out. Understand?"

She nodded. He kissed her forehead, then slid into the front seat and hunkered down.

TEN

Joss slid behind the wheel and fumbled with the keys, trembling so hard, she almost dropped them. She couldn't get the key into the slot. Dylan's hand covered hers, warm and strong, just like the first time she had wakened in the hospital.

"Lord." His low, smooth voice, so full of confidence, inspired calm to flow through her. "Lord, help us get Jason out. Guide us all to safety."

Peace filled Joss. She took a deep breath. Slid the key into the slot and started the car.

Turning on the headlights, she eased onto the road. Rocks crunched as she pulled around the corner, in full view of the house. Lights blazed from every window and Jason stood in the door. She breathed a sigh of relief. "He's still there," she whispered to Dylan.

"Good. Ease up to the door as we planned. But lower the windows first."

She punched the buttons on the door. All of the windows rolled down. She eased into the turn. Jason glanced back, took one step and then hesitated.

"He won't be able to walk backward and still keep his eyes on Vibora and his men. He's hesitating." She pulled up to the porch, then braked to a stop. "I'm going to get him."

"Joss...no." She was out of the door before Dylan's whisper reached her. She ran up to the porch. "I'm right here, Jason."

He glanced back when she grabbed his arm and squeezed. "I almost wish you'd gotten in that car and driven away." He nudged toward the gang. "They said you would."

She glared at Vibora. "They don't know anything about love. I'd never abandon you. You never left me."

He glanced down. She would remember the look in his eyes forever—full of apologies for betraying the cause of justice she'd worked so long and hard to preserve. Thankfulness for understanding his need to protect Maria and her family...and for Joss's forgiveness. It all flashed in his eyes in that one moment. She slid her hand down his arm and squeezed his hand.

"Let's get out of here."

He nodded once.

"One more step and you're off the porch." Joss prompted. "Just two steps on the dirt to the car."

As they stepped away, Vibora and Caulder moved closer, filling the doorway and blocking the light. From the corner of her eye, she caught movement as two more men moved into the large-paned front window. At least six guns were pointed right at them. Without a doubt more were hidden in the darkness.

Joss caught her breath but didn't waver. She released

Jason's hand long enough to open the car door, careful not to move in front of him or block his view of the men in the door. He slid slowly and carefully into the back seat, making sure not to lower his arm. Joss slammed the door and ran around the front of the car. She heard steps, knew Caulder and Vibora had stepped onto the porch, but she never looked to see how close they were. Her spine tingled. She could feel the gun sights pinpointing their marks.

She slid behind the wheel and yanked the car into gear. Only then did she dare glance at the door. Vibora was so angry, he was vibrating. Caulder had a hand on his shoulder, trying to hold him back.

She hit the gas and the tires ground into the dirt, kicking dust up and over the porch. Vibora screamed a curse and she heard running steps. A gun exploded. Dylan popped up.

"What—" Jason's startled gasp came from the back seat, but his words were drowned out by gunshots. The men on the porch fired at them.

Glass shattered. Gunfire blazed across the night. Joss turned the vehicle in a tight circle and headed to the road. She turned so sharply, she was sure two tires left the ground. Once the car straightened, she glanced into the rearview mirror. Vibora lay on the porch. Caulder was crouched in the dirt, in front, firing his pistol. Other gunmen stood beside him, with their weapons ablaze. Bullets pinged into the car and all around them.

The rear window shattered. She winced, ducked and turned around just as her headlights danced across the figure of a man running toward them. She was headed straight for him. She screamed and jerked the wheel to miss him as he lunged back. The car lurched sharply to the left. Jason cried out.

The explosives! Did I just kill us all?

Her foot dropped off the accelerator and she looked in the rearview window to see men running toward them and firing.

"Jason!"

"I'm fine. Go! Go! Go!"

She hit the gas and they sped out, kicking up dust and dirt again.

"Where are your agents? Why aren't they firing?" Joss yelled across the barrage of bullets coming their way.

"We must be in the way. They're afraid of hitting us."

"They should be. I've got enough explosives here to knock out all of these hills," Jason said from the back.

They were only feet from the corner when the night around them lit up with a thousand spotlights. A loud-speaker boomed across the night air.

"You're surrounded! Drop your weapons!"

Vibora's gang would never give up without a fight. Joss had the accelerator pressed to the floor already, or she would have hit it again. She wanted to be as far away as possible from the firestorm that was about to hit. Weapons fired one after the other, as if they were in a war zone. But thankfully they were clear.

Joss let out a sob as officers ran toward them. She eased off the gas and they coasted to a stop.

"Turn off the engine, Joss." She heard Dylan's soft command, but she couldn't make her body move. His strong hand on her arm finally jostled her into moving. She switched it off. Dylan turned in his seat.

"Jason, I'm Special Agent Dylan Murphy. I've been working with your sister. Let's get those explosives off you."

Joss looked in the mirror. Jason had his upraised arm and hand linked behind him. His fingers were wrapped around each other so tightly, she could see the whitened knuckles in the shadows of the car.

"I can get them off. There's an acid in this very fragile glass vial. All I have to do is slide it out of the explosive putty and we'll be safe. But first I need everyone to clear the area."

Joss shook her head. "I'm not leaving you."

"I'm not touching this until you are far away, Joss. Don't argue with me."

She started to protest, but Dylan grasped her arm. "I'll stay, Joss. He won't be alone."

He sat across from her, firm, strong, so certain in his promise. She would never love him more than she did right now. Still, she could lose both of them. Jason, because of his concern for humanity, and Dylan for his sense of duty.

She wanted to scream at both of them for being so willing to leave her. But she didn't. She climbed out of the car. An officer tried to assist her, but she jerked her arm loose and walked away.

She never looked back. Never paused. Her back itched, waiting for the explosion, but she refused to turn around or to halt. She kept walking past the officer, past the emergency vehicles and waiting technicians.

Why was everyone always so ready to leave her? Why didn't they want to stay with her as much as she wanted to stay with them? Why did the two men she loved most in the world always put duty first? Her heart ached with the old feelings of abandonment and aloneness.

An emergency technician caught up with her and tried to place a blanket around her shoulders. "Officer Walker, we need to check you out."

She shrugged off the blanket, let it drop to the ground and kept walking.

Why did her brother always attract needy people... people who dragged him away from her? Why couldn't she fall in love with a man who had a nine-to-five job...a man who would come home every night to sit on the couch, pet the million dogs they would have and maybe hold the babies?

She wanted her own home with things she loved. Things she chose and collected. Maybe even horses like Goldie and Patches. Babies! Her steps hitched. She wanted lots and lots of babies so she'd never be lonely again. Why couldn't someone love her enough for that?

Is it too much to ask, Lord? Why doesn't someone love me?

"Joss!" Dylan called her name, but she kept walking.

"We can't stop her. It's probably shock." She heard the technician's tense voice.

"I'll take care of her." Dylan's arms came around her. She tried to push them away, but they locked hard, pulling her against him.

"Joss, Jason is safe. He removed the vial. They're

cutting the duct tape and the explosives off his body. He'll be here in moments."

That voice. The voice that reached out to her in the darkness. The voice that dragged her back to reality. The voice that filled her with confidence, issued commands as easily as he drew breath. The voice that hummed and sang old hymns. Some of the lyrics came to her.

I once was lost, but now am found.

Another hymn echoed in Joss's thoughts.

God alone suffices.

Those words gave her pause. She thought she'd learned that lesson. God would never abandon or leave. He was always there.

"Joss!"

Jason pulled her into his arms. The familiar scent of his clothes and the cleaner he used to remove engine oil swept over her. He was alive. They were all alive. God had brought them through. So why had she so quickly forgotten Him?

Jason pushed her. "Joss, are you all right?" He gave her a little shake. "Jocelyn Walker, answer me!"

The grown-up tone he always used when she was in trouble. A rush of thankfulness that he was back and safe filled her. She hugged him fiercely. Then stepped away. "I'm fine."

But really she wasn't. *Things* were fine. They were safe. Vibora and his gang had been stopped. But she wasn't fine. She hadn't been fine for a long, long time. She'd regained her past, her memories. But somewhere she'd lost herself, her true self, the person God wanted her to be. That had happened many years ago. Maybe when she started chasing bad guys, trying to prove to herself that she was valuable…worthy of the sacrifices Jason made for her. God had taken second place to her career…to proving herself. And still He had not abandoned her. He'd been with her in every situation. In the tunnel. When He sent her Dylan. When Jason came to save her. When all of them made it out of that cul-de-sac alive. God had never left her side.

The emergency tech wrapped a blanket around her shoulders. "We need to check her out."

She was thankful when he bundled her up and guided her toward the ambulance. Thankful to be away from Dylan's puzzled frown and Jason's hurt expression. She needed time to think.

She sat on the step of the ambulance as the tech checked her out. Her mind whirled, puzzled over events. The tech ducked to get her attention. "You're definitely dehydrated, and those cuts on your wrists may need stitches."

She nodded but didn't say a word. He helped her inside and strapped her onto the gurney. As he closed the doors, she heard him mumble something about shock to Dylan and Jason. Then the doors slid closed on their troubled faces.

Dylan punched the end button on his cell phone and set it on his desk. His superiors wanted to debrief him in Washington. They considered his investigation a success.

Vibora was dead, killed in that first barrage of gun-fire on the porch. Dylan had shot him in the arm and injured him, but he'd risen later to fight in the gun battle with the officers on the hill. A long-range rifle shot had finally ended his life. Caulder was also dead, as well as many of the gang's captains, including Snake Man.

Lena Jones had entered the witness protection program with her family. Her testimony, along with that of Jason Walker, would put the remaining leaders behind bars. Jason would also enter the witness protection program, along with Maria Martinez, her mother and the youngest sister, at least until the trial. Dylan was taking no chance of someone connected to the gang rising up to take action against the Martinez family. Besides, their protection was part of the agreement he'd made with Jason in exchange for his information.

Jason's insights had been invaluable in rounding up those even remotely connected with the gang. Dylan's mission was over. But the price had been high. Maybe too high. Many people dead. Two gunfights in popu-lated cities. Seven people entering the protection program, not to mention the property damage to the gang house and Joss's apartment. Those issues needed to be ad-dressed and accounted for. His sterling reputation had been slightly tarnished by the high cost in lives and property. That bothered Dylan, but not as much as it should. What bothered him most was the change in Joss.

On the mountain he'd prayed that God would keep Joss safe. When he found her alive, all he wanted to do was snatch her up and hold her forever. But Joss had put distance between them. She'd pushed him to arm's length and kept him there in the days that had followed her release from the hospital.

At first he thought it was shock, but as the days wore on and her coolness continued, he wondered if she was suffering from post-traumatic stress disorder.

Her apartment was in shambles. He offered her the bedroom at the ranch, but she refused, so he arranged for her to stay with her brother, in the apartment they'd set up for him. She still refused to spend even a quiet moment with Dylan. He had so much to say to her, but she wouldn't let him near. She told him her brother would be leaving soon and she needed to spend as much time with him as she could.

Dylan respected that, but he also came to believe she was disappointed in him. Now that her brother and her memory had returned, the moments and feelings they'd shared weren't as important to her. And even worse he wasn't the man she'd believed him to be. He'd failed to protect her. He wanted to apologize, to tell her how wrong he had been. How right she was. But she wouldn't give him even a moment to do it.

Maybe he deserved it. Was it possible he had always been full of himself and his capabilities? Is that why Beth never came to him, never admitted her addiction? Maybe he had failed his little sister in ways he had never imagined...like he had Joss.

He'd let her down, and when it counted the most, failed her completely. Practically handed her over to the gang. She had every right to be disgusted with him. He was disgusted with himself. The most important case of his career and he'd made some serious missteps...

and probably forever alienated the most important person in his life.

He dreaded going to Washington. Even if his boss thought he'd succeeded, he knew, deep down, that he'd failed in the ways that counted most to him. But that didn't mean he couldn't make things right. Now. Before he left. Today Jason Walker was being transported to Maria and her family. Dylan was scheduled to meet with Holmquist and Joss to escort Walker to his flight.

Dylan would apologize to Joss at the airport, try to make things right before he left. He grabbed his phone and headed out the door.

Holmquist was waiting outside the terminal. "You look terrible."

"I just got off the phone with Washington."

"I see. They've been raking you over the coals."

"No, but they should. I deserve it."

Holmquist shook his head and moved toward the entrance doors. "I warned you."

"And I didn't listen. I know. It's my own fault."

They headed to the escalators. "Yeah, well, at least I didn't lose my best agent. Joss wants to start work next week. She needs time to find a new apartment and get settled."

Dylan paused. "You think she's ready?"

"Why? You don't think she's up to a return?"

He shrugged. "She seems different."

Holmquist turned away. "Yeah, I've noticed she's not treating you the same. Seems you fell off your pedestal."

"I didn't want to be on a pedestal. I knew I didn't deserve it."

"Doubt. That's the first honest emotion I've seen in you, Murphy. Maybe there's hope for you after all." He strode off, leaving Dylan shaking his head and hurrying to catch up.

He checked in at the airline desk, where he'd hired a private flight. He was taking no chances on Walker's safety. It would be months before they rounded up everyone connected with the Serpientes. They needed to make sure no one tried to step into the gap created by the loss of its leaders. In the meantime, Dylan wanted Jason and the Martinez family under protection. He'd fly with Joss's brother and reconnect him with Maria and her family. Once they were reunited, Dylan would hand them over to the agents of WITSEC. It would be the last he'd see of the man to whom he owed so much. Without Walker, Joss would be dead.

Behind him, an elevator opened. He turned. Gonzalez and several other agents exited, followed by Joss and Jason Walker. Joss gripped her brother's arm and smiled up at him. She looked at peace. Sad but calm, and more beautiful than Dylan remembered. Her unfettered hair flowed over the shoulders of a simple summer dress, white with bold red flowers splashed across it.

She hugged Holmquist and waved at Dylan. Just a slight wave of recognition. Not the smile in her eyes, the one he was used to seeing…and had come to expect.

She turned to her brother and wrapped her arms around him.

"I'll send word through the agency," Walker said.

Joss kissed him on the cheek. He turned and walked toward Dylan.

"I'll meet you inside."

Walker entered the loading ramp. Dylan nodded to Gonzalez as he walked by. The agent had done so much to help solve this case, he deserved to see the finish, so he was traveling with them to Colorado.

Joss stood nearby. Holmquist had his arm around her shoulders. Her hands clenched each other but her features were smooth and calm. When Holmquist saw Dylan walking toward them, he said something to Joss and headed to the elevator.

She stood across from him. They were alone. Most of the agents had either entered the plane or walked to the elevator with Holmquist.

This was the closest he'd been to Joss since the night of the shoot-out.

Dylan took a deep breath. "Joss, I'm sorry I let you down. After all of my promises to keep you safe, to never let them get you, I took you to my ranch and essentially handed you to them on a platter. I failed you."

She shook her head and her dark hair shimmered in the sunlight coming from the terminal windows. "No. You didn't let me down. You gave me a glimpse of the real me."

Surprise washed over him. Of all the things he had expected her to say, that was the most unexpected. "What do you mean?"

She sighed. "Being at your ranch house meant a lot to me. It was the first time in my life I saw what a life like that could be…all the generations of Murphys living and dining there. Investing in the land. A home full of memories…all the things you've been trying to run from are all the things that I've been missing in my life. Losing my memory changed me, made me see what I was missing. I know what I want now. A home. A place to call my own, to *make* my own. I want to be surrounded by things and creatures that love me—dogs…animals…babies."

Hope sprang to life inside him. "Joss, I love you."

She shook her head and his hope flamed out. "I learned something about myself, Dylan. I learned what your old hymn says, that God alone suffices. Of course I need love and friends. But I also need to know Him better. I need to know that I'm His. I think as I learn how to be a princess of the King, I'll also learn not to need others so much. I'll truly know my own value. You need to learn that too, Dylan. You need to know what drives you, why everything else needs to take second place to your mission."

"You're not second place. You're important to me."

"I think maybe I am important to you. But that's not enough. I don't want to come second to anyone's earthly love, Dylan. I deserve to be first. I'll always come below your duty. You've been called to do something more. It's a grand thing. A wonderful thing. But I'll always wonder why you're leaving me again. I have to le— to let God be enough."

He shook his head. "I do love you, Joss. Don't doub

A wry tilt lifted her lips. "But you love your more."

"You love your job too. We can support each o in our work."

"I want more than that, Dylan. I want the thi

don't want. I want that ranch and the horses and the rides along the river. Tell me honestly, would you give up your work to stay at the ranch?"

He hesitated. He couldn't. Not yet. And then the truth hit him. After all of his promises to God to protect and hold her forever, his work still had a hold on him… almost like a prisoner.

Slowly she shook her head. "You don't have to answer. I wouldn't be surprised if you're already done here. You're probably packed up, ready to return to Washington, after you turn Jason over."

His lips parted and he looked away. He didn't want to admit that she was right.

She sagged slightly and looked at the ground. He wanted to pull her into his arms and hold her, to tell her it would be all right. But it wouldn't be. She spoke the truth. He couldn't give her what she wanted.

She placed her hand on his cheek. Reaching up, she pressed her cool lips to his. They were soft. She smelled cool and crisp, like summers on the swing, sprinklers twitching over the grass and cucumbers. Things he'd left behind a long time ago. Maybe forever.

"Goodbye, Dylan. I'll pray for success with all you do." She turned and walked out of his life.

ELEVEN

Driving along the freeway, Joss topped a bluff and looked out over the vast San Pedro River Valley.

Black clouds filled the sky in spots. Late September, and the monsoons were fading. Soon they would face the dry, pleasant months of winter. She smiled, thinking how much she would miss these summer storms.

How her life had changed!

She used to hate storms but now savored the dark clouds tipped with gold. Rays of sunshine fell in golden spots across the valley. Even if she was setting herself up for heartache, she'd be thankful for this final beautiful drive to the ranch.

She'd heard that Dylan was back in town, but was taken by surprise when he called and asked her to pay a visit. He wanted her to come because their last meeting had been so stilted…so many things had been left unsaid.

It wasn't true. They'd said everything that needed to be said. The weeks he'd been gone confirmed that for Joss. Now more than ever she knew what she wanted.

Her weeks of prayer had revealed what the Lord had planted in her heart. She loved her work. She would always be devoted to law enforcement, but more than that, she wanted a home, to be surrounded by people she loved. She never wanted to return to a life filled only with her work. And Dylan knew no other way to live.

She pulled off the highway, onto the dirt road leading to his ranch. As she came close, a smile teased her lips. Patches and Goldie were tied out front. Dylan came out the front door, wearing his typical ranch wardrobe— jeans, T-shirt and boots. His curly hair peeked out from beneath a new hat and he looked so good, Joss's heart began to pound.

In his hands he carried the tan hat she'd worn before. She stopped the car and slid out.

"Hi."

"Hello." She shut the car door carefully, waiting for the hammering in her heart to stop. "I didn't expect you to return from Washington so soon...actually ever."

He slid the hat around his fingers. "I needed to make a decision about these animals." Joss's heart plummeted. So, he was selling them to his neighbor, Hank. That's why he'd returned. The only reason. The double-time beat of her heart slowed to a crawl.

She wished she had the money to buy Goldie and Patches. They meant a lot to her. But she didn't. She was saving to buy her own home. Not a wonderful place like this, just a house she could call her own. She didn't want to say that out loud, didn't want to share those hopes with Dylan. It would be too painful a reminder.

"I thought we might go for a ride."

She didn't think she could stand it, to ride beside him, to feel the horses and see the river. To think about what might have been. He should say what he thought needed to be said right here, so she could be on her way.

"A ride isn't a good idea."

He nodded. "Too many bad memories."

She gave a small laugh. "Too many good ones. I guess you've finally decided to cut all ties."

He smiled. "Not exactly. I had a long talk with my parents and changed my mind."

She studied him. "Really?"

"Yeah. They're staying here at the ranch for a while."

"Do they want to move back in?"

"Not exactly."

Frustrated, she gripped the keys in her hand. "Well, what exactly is going on? Why did you ask me to come here?"

"I have to get the place fixed up a bit. I need to buy some new furniture. Hang some pictures. I thought you might be willing to help."

She shook her head in disbelief at his callous disregard for her feelings. "I can't help you pick out your furnishings. You have to choose what *you* want."

He stepped closer. "No, hotshot. You need to buy the things you want. You said you needed to be surrounded by the things you love."

Her heart skipped a beat. "But they wouldn't be surrounding me."

"They would if I have my way."

She shook her head. "You've said time and again this won't work, Dylan, and now I agree. I heard you got a commendation and promotion, so you'll be heading back to Washington."

"Did you also hear I refused it? I asked to be transferred here as the area lead."

"You...you turned it down?"

"I had to tie up loose ends and think. You were right...about everything. My guilt was like the gray mist you described from your memory loss. I couldn't see anything beyond that gray wall of guilt."

He shook his head. "I couldn't accept the Lord's mercy because I was so certain I was unforgivable."

He reached for her with his free hand and grasped her fingertips. "Then I failed you on the mountain. All of my success as an agent, all of my accomplishments, meant nothing. I wanted to die."

"Oh, Dylan, I'm so sorry."

"I'm not. It was only when I was beaten and lost that I saw the truth. A second chance came to me, from your brother, the one I blamed the most. I realized that God's mercy is free for all of us. And it's much stronger and greater than we can imagine.

"It was like my eyes were opened. I realized what a beautiful gift the Lord had given me...something to chase away the dark. I had the future in my hands... my arms, and I didn't know what to do with it. I won't make that mistake again."

Her heart started pounding again. "But...but they're giving you more power. The ability to stop gangs everywhere. It's what you've always wanted."

He fit the cowboy hat onto her head. "Maybe that's what I *wanted*. But everything I really *need* is right here.

This ranch. Dogs. Maybe some more horses in that field over there." He moved closer. "Babies."

The jackhammer in her heart stopped and stuttered. "You...you need a momma for that job."

Reaching across the space, he slid his fingers through her hair and flipped it behind her shoulders. Then he tossed the hat aside and laid his hands on each side of her face. "I know. I've found the perfect one...if she'll have me."

He leaned in and pressed his lips to hers. He smelled so good. Like warm cotton and leather. His lips firm and certain, he kissed her until her knees were weak.

But he broke the kiss, wrapped his arms around her, tucked her head into the curve of his neck and whispered, "I was like you, Joss. I needed to know where the Lord really wanted me to be. I figured out that's right here, beside you. Will you marry me? Will you help me make a home, and help me give dogs and horses grown-up names?"

She wrapped her arms around his neck. "Yes," she murmured. "On one condition...that we always make our home here, where all of the Murphys have lived. I want our babies to know who they are and where they come from. I don't ever want them to feel lost like we did."

He kissed her again, long and hard, until thunder boomed overhead.

Dylan pulled back. "Come on. My parents are anxious to meet you. Besides, we need to get you inside before this storm starts."

Too late. The clouds let loose and buckets of water

poured over them. Smiling, Joss pulled him close for another kiss.

"I'm fine right where I am. I'm not afraid. Good things happen after storms."

* * * * *

Dear Reader,

I grew up on the coast of California, with lots of green and the beach. When I married, we moved to the Mojave Desert. When we came over the mountains and I looked down on our brown, flat desert home, I began to cry. My husband hurried to say, "It's okay. You can live with your parents and I'll come home on the weekends."

Of course, we all know that's not how a marriage works, and our three years turned into thirty-seven. So I was ready for a change. My husband's next job sent us to the Arabian Desert. I thought the Mojave was so barren, it looked like the lunar landscape. Then I saw the Empty Quarter of Oman, a true lunar landscape, where nothing lives and the land is so flat, you can see a truck on the road, a hundred miles away.

When we moved to Southern Arizona, I discovered a wonderland of plants, such as the humanlike saguaros, thousands of blooming cacti and unique animals called javelinas. Nothing can match skies that turn to fire at sunset or the summer monsoon rains that drop down suddenly, like a curtain of water.

As you can see, I've come to accept the Lord's plan for me to be a "desert rat." I fell in love with the Sonoran Desert and decided I had to write a story set there. I hope you love it too.

Blessings!
Tanya Stowe

SPECIAL EXCERPT FROM

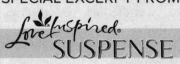

Love Inspired.
SUSPENSE

*When a rookie K-9 cop becomes the target of a
dangerous stalker, can she stay one step ahead of this
killer with the help of her boss and his K-9 partner?*

Read on for a sneak preview of
Courage Under Fire *by Sharon Dunn,*
the next exciting installment to the
True Blue K-9 Unit miniseries, available in
October 2019 from Love Inspired Suspense.

Rookie K-9 officer Lani Branson took in a deep breath as
she pedaled her bike along the trail in the Jamaica Bay
Wildlife Refuge. Water rushed and receded from the shore
just over the dunes. The high-rises of New York City,
made hazy from the dusky twilight, were visible across
the expanse of water.

She sped up even more.

Tonight was important. This training exercise was an
opportunity to prove herself to the other K-9 officers who
waited back at the visitors' center with the tracking dogs
for her to give the go-ahead. Playing the part of a child lost
in the refuge so the dogs could practice tracking her was
probably a less-than-desirable duty for the senior officers.

Reaching up to her shoulder, Lani got off her bike and
pressed the button on the radio. "I'm in place."

The smooth tenor voice of her supervisor, Chief Noah Jameson, came over the line. "Good—you made it out there in record time."

Up ahead she spotted an object shining in the setting sun. She jogged toward it. A bicycle, not hers, was propped against a tree.

A knot of tension formed at the back of her neck as she turned in a half circle, taking in the area around her. It was possible someone had left the bike behind. Vagrants could have wandered into the area.

She studied the bike a little closer. State-of-the-art and in good condition. Not the kind of bike someone just dumped.

A branch cracked. Her breath caught in her throat. Fear caused her heartbeat to drum in her ears.

"NYPD." She hadn't worn her gun for this exercise. Her eyes scanned all around her, searching for movement and color. "You need to show yourself."

Seconds ticked by. Her heart pounded.

Someone else was out here.

Don't miss
Courage Under Fire *by Sharon Dunn,*
available October 2019 wherever
Love Inspired® Suspense books and ebooks are sold.

www.LoveInspired.com

LISEXP0919